FREE TO BE... YOU AND ME

Conceived by Marlo Thomas

Developed and Edited by Carole Hart,
Letty Cottin Pogrebin, Mary Rodgers
and Marlo Thomas

Editor: Francine Klagsbrun
Art Director: Samuel N. Antupit

A project of the Ms. Foundation, Inc.

BANTAM BOOKS
TORONTO · NEW YORK · LONDON · SYDNEY · AUCKLAND

FREE TO BE...YOU AND ME

A Bantam Book/published by arrangement with the author

PRINTING HISTORY
McGraw Hill Book Co. edition published 1974, a project of the MS.
Foundation, Inc.

Acknowledgments:

Words and music for "Free to Be...You and Me," "When We Grow Up," "Sisters and Brothers," and "Helping," copyright © 1972 Ms. Foundation for Women, Inc. Used by permission.

Words and music for "Parents Are People," "It's All Right To Cry," and "Glad To Have a Friend Like You" and words for "Housework" and "My Dog Is a Plumber," copyright © 1972 Free To Be Foundation, Inc.

"Atalanta," copyright © 1973 Free To Be Foundation, Inc.

"William's Doll," adapted from the book *William's Doll* by Charlotte Zolotow. Text copyright © 1972 Charlotte Zolotow. Used by permission of Harper & Row, Publishers, Inc. Words and music for adaptation, copyright © 1972 Ms. Foundation for Women, Inc.

"Dudley Pippin and the Principal," by Phil Ressner, adapted from "Dudley and the Principal" from the book *Dudley Pippin* by Phil Ressner, illustrated by Arnold Lobel. Text copyright © 1965 Phil Ressner. Pictures copyright © 1965 Arnold Lobel. Reprinted by permission of Harper & Row, Publishers, Inc.

"How I Crossed the Street for the First Time All By Myself," by Herb Gardner, copyright © 1955 Herb Gardner. Reprinted by permission.

"Three Wishes," by Lucille Clifton, copyright © 1974 Lucille Clifton. Used by permission of the author and Curtis Brown, Ltd.

Photographs for "Parents Are People" and "It's All Right To Cry" from United Press International. Photograph of Marlo Thomas and friends by Kenn Duncan, furnished courtesy of Bell Records.

Piano arrangements for this book by Stephen Lawrence.

Bantam edition/December 1987

Note: The music in this book is designed to be played by children of all ages, shapes, sizes, colors, and sexes. Some of the songs are easy to play. Some are more challenging. In either case, chord names above the notes can be used to improvise simpler (or more complex) arrangements of the pieces. Even if you cannot read music, you can enjoy the poems and stories within the musical scores.

Library of Congress Cataloging-in-Publication Data

Free to be...you and me.

Reprint. Originally published: New York : McGraw-Hill, 1974 as a project of the Ms. Foundation.
Summary: A number of stories, poems, and songs which demonstrate that people can choose to do or be whatever they desire.
1. Children's literature.   [1. Short stories.
2. American poetry—Collections.   3. Songs]   I. Thomas, Marlo.   II. Ms. Foundation for Women (U.S.)
PZ5.F86   1987   [Fic]   87-31821
ISBN 0-553-34544-3 (pbk.)

Published simultaneously in the United States and Canada

Bantam Books are published by Bantam Books, a division of Bantam Double-day Dell Publishing Group, Inc. Its trademark, consisting of the words "Bantam Books" and the portrayal of a rooster, is Registered in U.S. Patent and Trademark Office and in other countries. Marca Registrada. Bantam Books, 666 Fifth Avenue, New York, New York 10103.

PRINTED IN THE UNITED STATES OF AMERICA

KP   0 9 8 7 6 5 4 3 2 1

Contents

This Is the Foreword...

   . . . which means you've just gotten this book, so the pages are still clean and unbent and unmarked, the cover is still shiny and still on—all the usual signs of a book that doesn't belong to anybody yet. What I want very much to see, in a year or so, is a wreck of a book—not so wrecked that it can't be read, but the kind of wreck which means it *has* been read; borrowed, reread, sung, felt and understood. A book that has been touched and that has touched you.

   Let me tell you how this book started. It started very small; about three feet tall—the height of my niece Dionne a year and a half ago when she asked me to read her a bedtime story. I was saddened to find that all of her books were just *that,* books that put her and her mind to sleep. I started to look through stores and found shelf after shelf of books that told boys and girls who they should be, who they ought to be, but seldom who they *could* be.

   I wanted a book for Dionne, a special book, a party of a book, to celebrate who she was and who she could be, all the possibilities and all the possible Dionnes. I've always believed that anybody could be anything, especially me. I wanted Dionne to feel that way. And I want you to feel that way too. I found that many of my writer and poet friends felt as I did about the children they loved, and these wonderfully talented and generous people

have donated their work to this idea—a book of stories and poems and songs that would help boys and girls feel free to be who they are and who they want to be.

As many of you may know, some of these stories and songs became a record album on their way to being a book. I'm pleased that there's a record and we enjoyed putting it together; but I must admit that it is now, as a book, what I had always wanted it to be. We were able to include many more things in the book, but mostly—and I know I'm putting myself out of a job here—the only actor or singer a book needs is you. The words and pictures are yours to say and to see in your own way. Each story changes with the voice that tells it, each picture with the eyes that see it. A book is yours to read aloud and act out and sing in person; and the person is you.

I want this book to belong to you; and even more I want you who read this book to belong to yourselves. We have made this book in the hope that it will start you a few steps, or a leap, in that direction. Those of you who are looking for Wonderland or Prince Charming or a sleeping or even sleepy princess will not find them here. The world we care about here is the most adventurous, the largest, the most wondrous of all; the world of feeling and the land of ourselves.

So, Dionne and all of you—take a giant step.

May I?

Yes, you may.

Yes, we hope you will.

—Marlo Thomas

What Buying This Book Will Do

The book you are holding in your hands right now is unique in many ways. Most of them you will see by reading and looking, but one of the most important differences can't be seen at all. That is where the money is going; a big part of the money you paid when you bought this book.

The proud creators of *Free To Be . . . You and Me*—those who conceived of the project along with the writers and artists and poets and musicians and all those many people who worked long and lovingly to put it together—care about its message so much that they decided not to take their usual royalties from any profits that might result. Instead, that potential money has been contributed to the Ms. Foundation for Women, Inc., which will support a variety of educational projects aimed at improving the skills, conditions and status of women and children. This means developing new kinds of learning materials, child care centers, health care services, teaching techniques, information and referral centers and much more: all the concrete ways in which this book's message of freedom can be realized and all the practical changes that are necessary to get rid of old-fashioned systems based on sex and race.

So you see, this is a project born of love and hope. Our only regret is that *Free To Be . . . You and Me* and the change it reflects weren't part of our own childhoods. But then, the children we once were are inside us still—and so this very different book delights us all.

—Gloria Steinem

A Note to Parents and Other Grown-up Friends:

You are about to share an extraordinary and memorable experience with the children in your life.

Free To Be . . . You and Me is a new form of entertainment. It is a book of adventure because it opens new possibilities for growth and change. It is a book of humor—but the laugh is on old constraints and worn-out conventions. It is also a song book and a story book, a collection of poems and a gallery of pictures that extol the natural child in all of us.

But this happy hodge-podge has actually been conceived with great care. Life-enhancing themes of autonomy and interdependence may be found skillfully blended with the wonder and the wit. There are important messages within the merriment.

Some of the selections are designed to expand children's personal horizons so that they can invent their own futures without limitation. Other selections dispel the myths that distort reality—like pretty-equals-good, and all-mothers-stay-in-the-kitchen, and big-boys-don't-cry.

Several pieces in the book challenge stereotypes that have imprisoned children's imaginations, stunted their emotional development and restricted the games, toys and people they play with. And two or three selections redefine fairy tales so that Sleeping Beauty can stay awake and look at her life with her eyes wide open, and the brave prince can relax and enjoy *his* life without continually having to prove his "manhood."

Parents and friends of children are always searching for stories that we can read without embarrassment, and poetry that can be recited without cynicism or excessive explanation. In the process we've learned what will delight a child and what we all can do without.

We want fantasy without illusion; stories of excitement without cruelty or violence; songs that we can sing together without condescension; and artwork that appeals without patronizing. What we have been seeking is a literature of human diversity that celebrates choice and that does not exclude any child from its pleasures because of race or sex, geography or family occupation, religion or temperament.

These same values have been uppermost in the minds of the first-rate writers and artists who have contributed to this book. Perhaps that is why love and vitality shine from every page.

If you stop and think about it you'll find something here about brotherhood that includes sisterhood, and about cooperation and friendship, and about mutual respect and personal dignity.

But if you don't stop to think about it, you'll find pure entertainment that will bring exuberant joy into your classroom or living room. So grab a guitar, sit down at the piano or snuggle with someone at bedtime and start enjoying this book. There's something in it for the free spirit in every adult and the wise soul in every child.

—Letty Cottin Pogrebin

Free to Be...You and Me

There's a land that I see
Where the children are free.
And I say it ain't far
To this land, from where we are.

Take my hand. Come with me,
Where the children are free.
Come with me, take my hand,
And we'll live . . .

In a land
Where the river runs free—
(In a land)
Through the green country—
(In a land)
To a shining sea.

And you and me
Are free to be
You and me.

I see a land, bright and clear,
And the time's coming near,
When we'll live in this land,
You and me, hand-in-hand.

Take my hand. Come along,
Lend your voice to my song.
Come along. Take my hand,
Sing a song . . .

Music by Stephen Lawrence
Lyric by Bruce Hart

For a land
Where the river runs free—
(For a land)
Through the green country—
(For a land)
To a shining sea—
(For a land)
Where the horses run free.

And you and me
Are free to be
You and me.

Every boy in this land
Grows to be his own man.
In this land, every girl
Grows to be her own woman.

Take my hand. Come with me,
Where the children are free.
Come with me. Take my hand,
And we'll run . . .

To a land
Where the river runs free—
(To a land)
Through the green country—
(To a land)
To a shining sea—
(To a land)
Where the horses run free—
(To a land)
Where the children are free.

And you and me
Are free to be
You and me.

And you and me
Are free to be
You and me.

With spirit

There's a (1) land that I see_____ where the chil - dren are free,_____
(2) land, bright and clear,_____ and the time's_____ com - in' near,_____

_____ and I say_____ it ain't far_____ to this land_____ from where we are._____
when we'll live_____ in this land,_____ you and me_____ hand - in - hand._____

18

21

3RD CHORUS

   Eb/G   F7/A Bb
    Ev - 'ry boy in this land
           F
    Grows to be his own man.
         C   Eb
    In this land, ev'ry girl
          Bb   Bb F
    Grows to be her own wo - man.
   Bb
    Take my hand, come with me,
            F
    Where the children are free.
         C   Eb
    Come with me, take my hand,
          Bb
    And we'll run...

         F   Bb   F
    To a land where the river runs free,
    Bb   F   Bb   F
    To a land through the green country,
    Bb   F   Bb   F
    To a land to a shining sea
    Bb   F   Bb   F
    To a land where the horses run free
    Bb   F   Bb   F
    To a land where the children are free.
            Am   F7   Bb
    And you and me are free to be
  C7sus4   F(Bb, F, Bb, F, Bb, F)
    You and me.

(Note: The third chorus may be sung in the original key (E), or ½ tone higher
        (F), for which chord names are given here.)

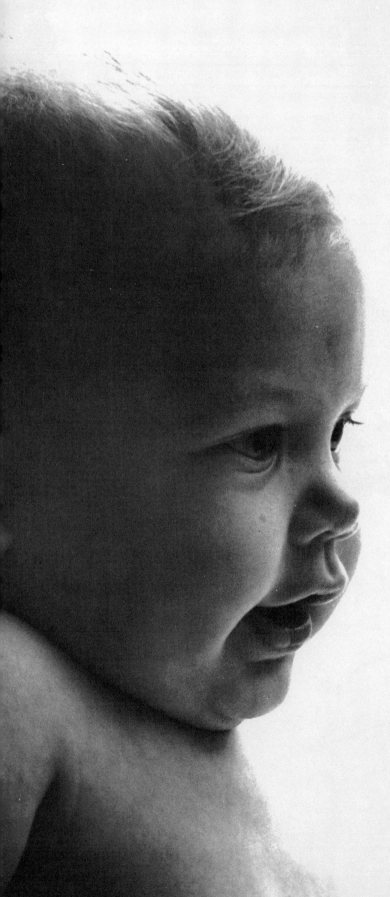

Boy Meets Girl

by Peter Stone and Carl Reiner

DEEP VOICE: Hi!

HIGH VOICE: Hi.

DEEP VOICE: I'm a baby.

HIGH VOICE: What do you think I am, a loaf of bread?

DEEP VOICE: You could be—what do I know? I'm just born. I'm a baby. I don't even know if I'm under a tree or in a hospital or what. I'm just so glad to be here.

HIGH VOICE: Well, I'm a baby, too.

DEEP VOICE: Have it your own way. I don't want to fight about it.

HIGH VOICE: What are you, scared?

DEEP VOICE: Yes, I am. I'm a little scared. I'll tell you why. See, I don't know if I'm a boy or a girl yet.

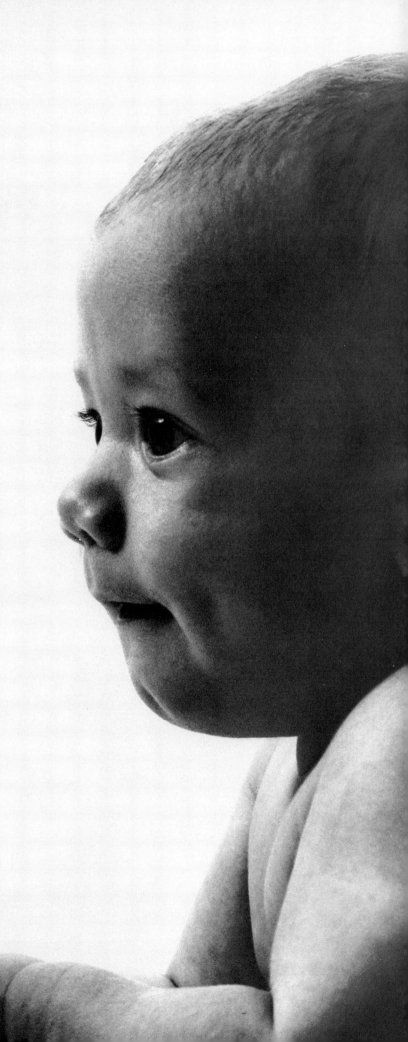

HIGH VOICE: What's that got to do with it?

DEEP VOICE: Well, if you're a boy and I'm a girl you can beat me up. Do you think I want to lose a tooth my first day alive?

HIGH VOICE: What's a tooth?

DEEP VOICE: Search me. I'm just born. I'm a baby. I don't know nothing yet.

HIGH VOICE: Do you think you're a girl?

DEEP VOICE: I don't know. I might be. I think I am. I've never been anything before. Let me see. Let me take a little look around. Hmm. Cute feet. Small, dainty. Yup, yup, I'm a girl. That's it. Girltime.

HIGH VOICE: What do you think I am?

DEEP VOICE: You? That's easy—you're a boy.

HIGH VOICE: Are you sure?

DEEP VOICE: Of course I'm sure. I'm alive already four, five minutes and I haven't been wrong yet.

HIGH VOICE: Gee, I don't feel like a boy.

DEEP VOICE: That's because you can't see yourself.

HIGH VOICE: Why? What do I look like?

DEEP VOICE: Bald. You're bald fellow. Bald, bald, bald. You're bald as a ping-pong ball. Are you bald!

HIGH VOICE: So?

DEEP VOICE: So, boys are bald and girls have hair.

HIGH VOICE: Are you sure?

DEEP VOICE: Of course, I'm sure. Who's bald, your mother or your father?

HIGH VOICE: My father.

DEEP VOICE: I rest my case.

HIGH VOICE: Hmm. You're bald, too.

DEEP VOICE: You're kidding!

HIGH VOICE: No, I'm not.

DEEP VOICE: Don't look!

HIGH VOICE: Why?

DEEP VOICE: A bald girl—blech!—disgusting!

HIGH VOICE: Maybe you're a boy and I'm a girl.

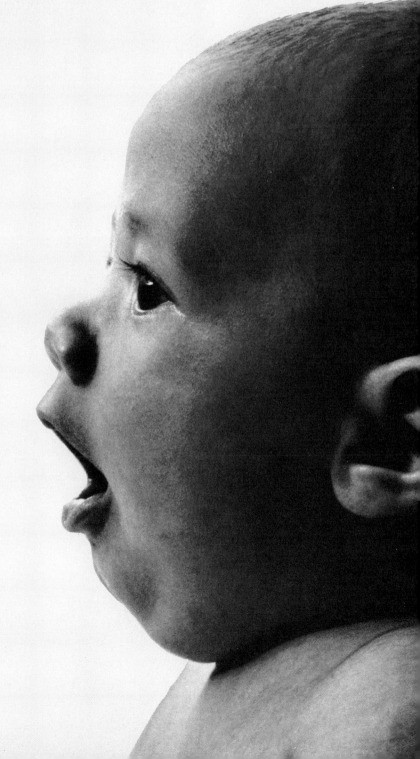

DEEP VOICE: There you go again. I told you—I'm a girl. I know it. I know it. I'm a girl, and you're a boy.

HIGH VOICE: I think you're wrong.

DEEP VOICE: I am never wrong! What about shaving?

HIGH VOICE: What about it?

DEEP VOICE: You just shaved, right?

HIGH VOICE: Wrong.

DEEP VOICE: Exactly! And you know why? Because everyone's born with a clean shave. It's just that girls keep theirs and boys don't.

HIGH VOICE: So, what does that prove?

DEEP VOICE: Tomorrow morning, the one that needs a shave, he's a boy.

HIGH VOICE: I can't wait until tomorrow morning.

DEEP VOICE: See? That proves it. Girls are patient, boys are impatient.

HIGH VOICE: Yeh? What else?

DEEP VOICE: Can you keep a secret?

HIGH VOICE: Absolutely.

DEEP VOICE: There you go—
boys keep secrets, girls don't.

HIGH VOICE: Go on.

DEEP VOICE: Are you afraid of mice?

HIGH VOICE: No.

DEEP VOICE: I am. I'm terrified of them. I hate them. Squeak. Squeak. Squeak. What do you want to be when you grow up?

HIGH VOICE: A fireman.

DEEP VOICE: What'd I tell you?

HIGH VOICE: How about you?

DEEP VOICE: A cocktail waitress. Does that prove anything to you?

HIGH VOICE: You must be right.

DEEP VOICE: I told you—I'm always right. You're a boy and I'm the girl.

HIGH VOICE: I guess so. Oh, wait—here comes the nurse to change our diapers.

DEEP VOICE: About time, too—I have never been so uncomfortable in my life.

HIGH VOICE: Hey—look at that!

DEEP VOICE: What?

HIGH VOICE: You see that? I *am* a girl—and you're a boy!

DEEP VOICE: Hey—it sure looks like it.

HIGH VOICE: What do you think of that?

DEEP VOICE: I can't understand it.

HIGH VOICE: Well, it sure goes to show you.

DEEP VOICE: What?

HIGH VOICE: You can't judge a book by its cover.

DEEP VOICE: Ha. Ha. Ha. What does that mean?

HIGH VOICE: How should I know? I'm only a baby.

DEEP VOICE: So am I. Goo.

HIGH VOICE: Goo.

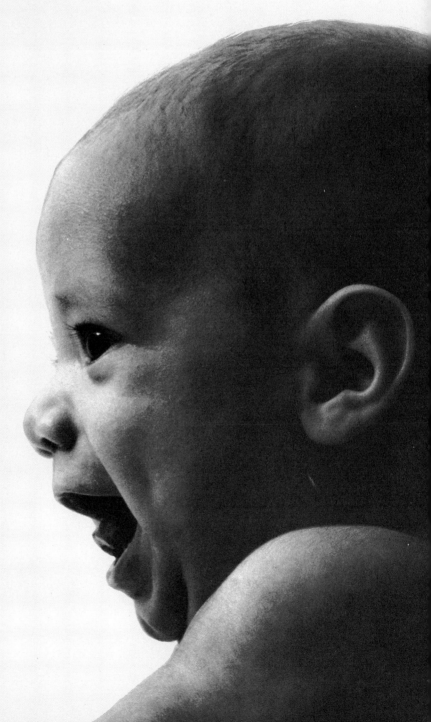

When We Grow Up

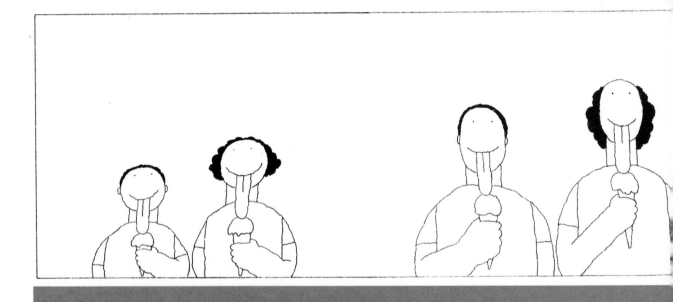

Music by Stephen Lawrence
Lyric by Shelley Miller

When we grow up will I be pretty?
Will you be big and strong?
Will I wear dresses that show off my knees?
Will you wear trousers twice as long?

Well, I don't care if I'm pretty at all
And I don't care if you never get tall
I like what I look like and you're nice small
We don't have to change at all.

When we grow up will I be a lady?
Will you be on the moon?
Well, it might be all right to dance by its light
But I'm gonna get up there soon.

Well, I don't care if I'm pretty at all
And I don't care if you never get tall
I like what I look like and you're nice small
We don't have to change at all.

When I grow up I'm going to be happy
And do what I like to do,
Like making noise and making faces
And making friends like you.

And when we grow up do you think we'll see
That I'm still like you
And you're still like me?
I might be pretty
You might grow tall
But we don't have to change at all.

When We Grow Up

nev - er get tall.___ I like what I look like, and you're nice small, we

don't have to change at all.

When I grow up I'm

go - ing to be hap-py and do what I like to do ___ like mak-ing noise and

What Are Little Boys Made Of?

by Elaine Laron
drawing by Max Burgle, age 7

What are little boys made of, made of?
What are little boys made of?
Love and care
And skin and hair
That's what little boys are made of.

What are little girls made of, made of?
What are little girls made of?
Care and love
And (SEE ABOVE)
That's what little girls are made of.

Ladies First

by Shel Silverstein
adapted by Mary Rodgers

Did you hear the one about the little girl who was a "tender sweet young thing?" Well, that's the way she thought of herself. And this tender sweet young thing spent a great deal of time just looking in the mirror, saying,

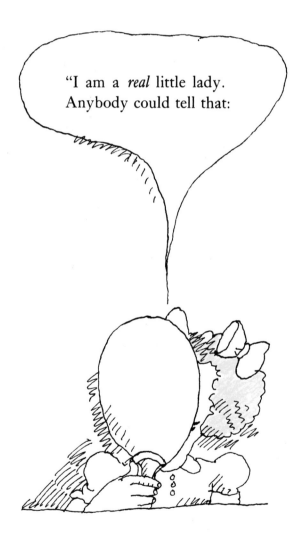

"I am a *real* little lady.
Anybody could tell that:

When she was at the end of the lunch line at school, all she had to say was,

"Ladies first, ladies first!"

and she'd get right up to the front of the line.

Well, her life went on like that
for quite awhile and she wound up
having a pretty good time—you know
—admiring herself in mirrors,
always getting to be first in line,
and stuff like that.

And then one day she went exploring with a whole group of other people through the wilds of a deep and beastly jungle. As she went along through the tangled trails and the prickly vines, she would say things like,

"I have got to be careful of my lovely
dress and my nice white socks
and my shiny, shiny shoes
and my curly, curly locks,
so
would somebody please
clear the way for me?"

And they did.

Or sometimes she'd say,

"What do you *mean* there aren't enough mangoes to go around
and I'll have to share my mango
because I was the last one across that icky river
full of crocodiles and snakes?
No matter how last I am,
it's still
'Ladies first, ladies first.'
so
hand over a whole mango, please."

And they did.

41

Well, then, guess what happened? Out of nowhere, the exploring party was seized, grabbed up by a bunch of hungry tigers, and these tigers tied all the people up and dragged them back to their tiger lair where they sniffed around, trying to decide what would make the best dinner.

"How about this one?"

said the tiger chief.

"Naah, too bony,"

said the others.

"What about this one? It's got a lotta meat on it."

"Uh-unh, meaty, but muscle-y."

"Oh for heavens sake, don't take all night!"

said the chief tiger.

"I never *saw* such a pack of picky eaters!

How about *this* one then? It looks tender, smells nice, in fact, I never saw anything quite like it before. I wonder what it is."

SNIFF SNIFF

"I am a tender, sweet young thing,"

"Oh, far out,"

she said.

said the tiger chief.

43

"I'm also a little lady.
You should know that by my lovely clothes and my
lovely smell. And if it's all the same to you, Tiger Tweetie,
I wish you'd stop licking me and untie me, this instant.
My dress is getting mussed."

"Yes . . . Well as a matter of fact, we were all just trying to decide who to
untie first."

"*Ladies* first, *ladies* first," she said.

And so she was.

And mighty tasty, too!

Don't Dress Your Cat in an Apron

by Dan Greenburg

Don't dress your cat in an apron
Just 'cause he's learning to bake.
Don't put your horse in a nightgown
Just 'cause he can't stay awake.
Don't dress your snake in a muu-muu
Just 'cause he's off on a cruise.
Don't dress your whale in galoshes
If she really prefers overshoes.

A person should wear what he wants to
And not just what other folks say.
A person should do what she likes to—
A person's a person that way.

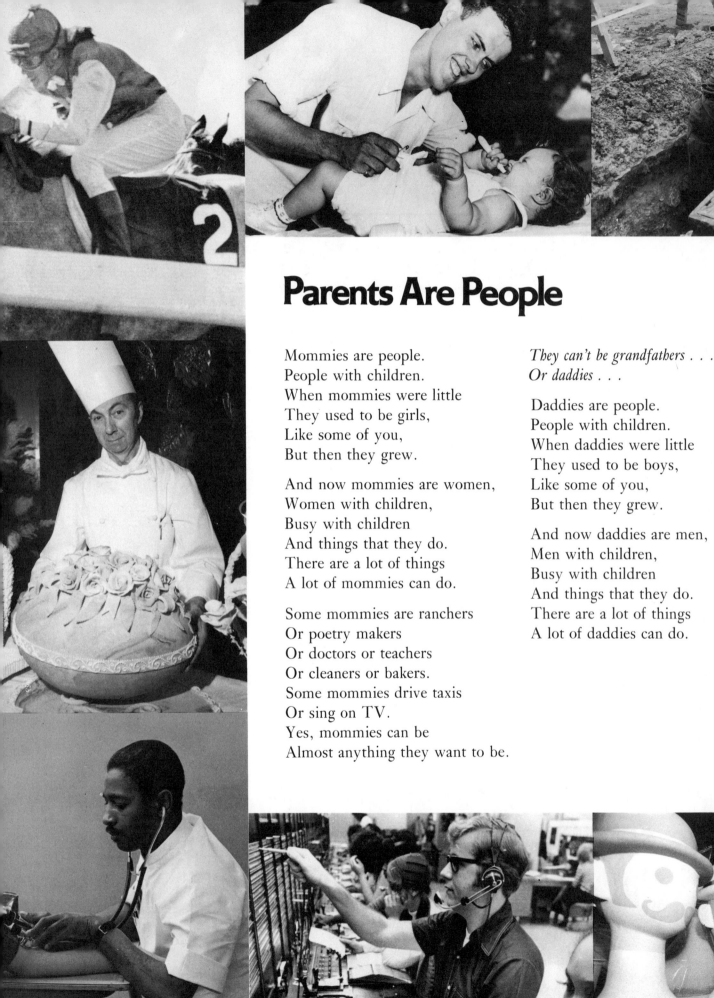

Parents Are People

Mommies are people.
People with children.
When mommies were little
They used to be girls,
Like some of you,
But then they grew.

And now mommies are women,
Women with children,
Busy with children
And things that they do.
There are a lot of things
A lot of mommies can do.

Some mommies are ranchers
Or poetry makers
Or doctors or teachers
Or cleaners or bakers.
Some mommies drive taxis
Or sing on TV.
Yes, mommies can be
Almost anything they want to be.

They can't be grandfathers . . .
Or daddies . . .

Daddies are people.
People with children.
When daddies were little
They used to be boys,
Like some of you,
But then they grew.

And now daddies are men,
Men with children,
Busy with children
And things that they do.
There are a lot of things
A lot of daddies can do.

by Carol Hall

Some daddies are writers
Or grocery sellers
Or painters or welders
Or funny joke tellers.
Some daddies play cello
Or sail on the sea.
Yes, daddies can be
Almost anything they want to be.

They can't be grandmas . . .
Or mommies . . .

Parents are people.
People with children.
When parents were little
They used to be kids,
Like all of you.
But then they grew.

And now parents are grown-ups,
Grown-ups with children,
Busy with children
And things that they do.
There are a lot of things
A lot of mommies
And a lot of daddies
And a lot of parents
Can do.

Parents Are People

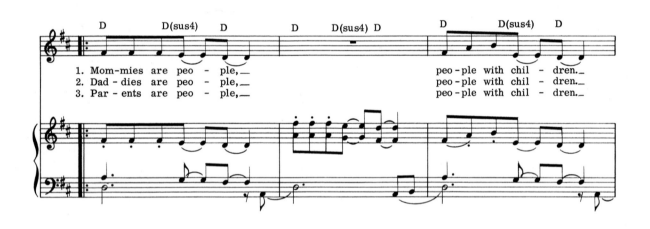

1. Mom - mies are peo - ple, ___ peo - ple with chil - dren. ___
2. Dad - dies are peo - ple, ___ peo - ple with chil - dren. ___
3. Par - ents are peo - ple, ___ peo - ple with chil - dren. ___

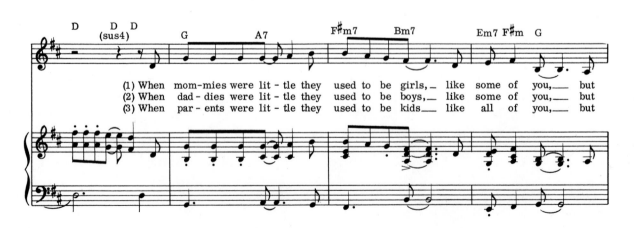

(1) When mom - mies were lit - tle they used to be girls, ___ like some of you, ___ but
(2) When dad - dies were lit - tle they used to be boys, ___ like some of you, ___ but
(3) When par - ents were lit - tle they used to be kids ___ like all of you, ___ but

then they grew. And now mom-mies are wo - men,   wo-men with chil - dren,
then they grew. And now dad - dies are men,   men with chil - dren,
then they grew. And now par - ents are grown-ups,   grown-ups with chil - dren,

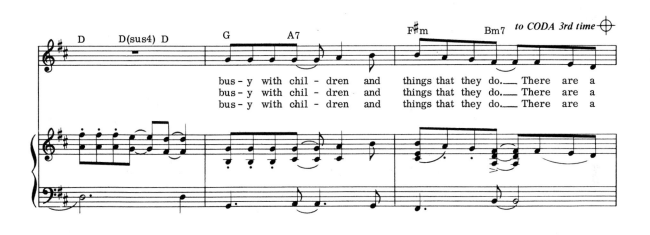

to CODA 3rd time

bus - y with chil - dren   and   things that they do.__ There are a
bus - y with chil - dren   and   things that they do.__ There are a
bus - y with chil - dren   and   things that they do.__ There are a

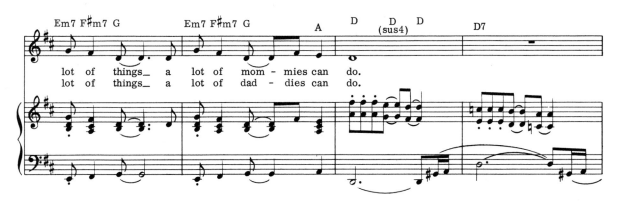

lot of things__ a   lot of   mom - mies can   do.
lot of things__ a   lot of   dad - dies can   do.

Some mom-mies are ranch-ers or po-et-ry mak-ers__ or
Some dad-dies are writ-ers or gro-cer-y sell-ers__ or

doc-tors or teach-ers or clean-ers or bak-ers.__ Some mom-mies drive tax-is or
paint-ers or weld-ers or fun-ny joke tell-ers.__ Some dad-dies play cel-lo or

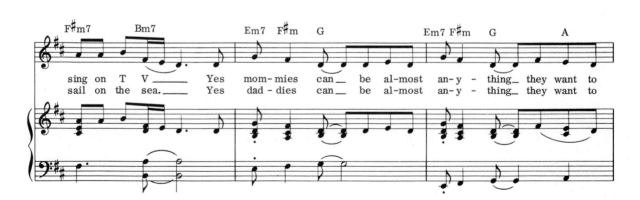

sing on T V__ Yes mom-mies can__ be al-most an-y-thing__ they want to
sail on the sea.__ Yes dad-dies can__ be al-most an-y-thing__ they want to

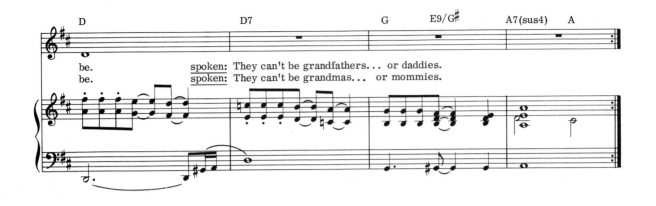

spoken: They can't be grandfathers... or daddies.
spoken: They can't be grandmas... or mommies.

CODA

lot of things_ a lot of mom - mies and a lot of dad - dies and a lot of par - ents can_

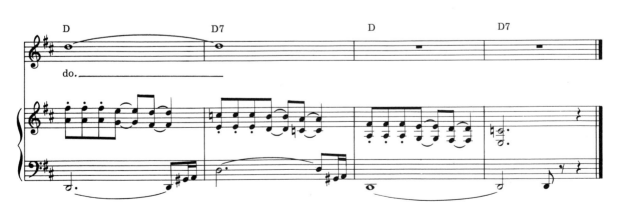

do.

Housework

by Sheldon Harnick

You know, there are times
    when we happen to be
just sitting there quietly
    watching TV,
when the program we're watching

will stop for awhile
and suddenly someone
    appears with a smile
and starts to show us
    how terribly urgent
it is to buy some brand
    of detergent
        or soap
        or cleanser
        or cleaner
        or powder
        or paste

or wax
or bleach—
to help with the housework.

Now, most of the time
it's a lady we see
who's doing the housework
on TV.
She's cheerfully scouring
a skillet or two,
or she's polishing pots
'til they gleam like new,

or she's scrubbing the tub,
or she's mopping the floors,
or she's wiping the stains
from the walls and the doors,
or she's washing the windows,
the dishes, the clothes,
or waxing the furniture
'til it just glows,
or cleaning the "fridge,"
or the stove or the sink
with a lighthearted smile
and a friendly wink

and she's doing her best
   to make us think
that *her* soap
      or detergent
      or cleanser
      or cleaner
      or powder
      or paste
      or wax
      or bleach
is the best kind of soap
      (or detergent

      or cleanser
      or cleaner
      or powder
      or paste
      or wax
      or bleach)
that there is in the whole wide world!

And maybe it is . . .
and maybe it isn't . . .
and maybe it does what they
   say it will do . . .

but I'll tell you one thing
   I *know* is true:

The lady we see
   when we're watching TV—
The lady who smiles
   as she scours
        or scrubs
        or rubs
        or washes
        or wipes
        or mops

        or dusts
        or cleans—
or whatever she does
on our TV screens—
that lady is smiling
because she's an actress.
And she's earning money
for learning those speeches
that mention those wonderful
        soaps
        and detergents
        and cleansers

and cleaners
and powders
and pastes
and waxes
and bleaches.
So the very next time
you happen to be
just sitting there quietly
watching TV,
and you see some nice lady
who smiles as

she scours
or scrubs
or rubs
or washes
or wipes
or mops
or dusts
or cleans
remember:
Nobody smiles doing housework
but those ladies you see on TV.
Because even if

the soap
    or detergent
    or cleanser
    or cleaner
    or powder
    or paste
    or wax
    or bleach
that you use
    is the very best one—
housework

    is just no fun.

Children,
when you have a house of your own
make sure, when there's housework to do,
that you don't have to do it alone.
Little boys, little girls,
when you're big husbands and wives,
if you want all the days of your lives
to seem sunny as summer weather
make sure, when there's housework to do,
that you do it together.

Helping

by Shel Silverstein

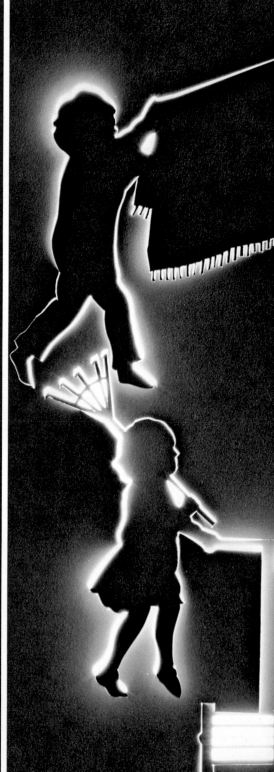

Jen-ni-fer Joy she made a toy, and Za-cha-ry Zugg helped break it.__ And

some kind of help is the kind of help that help-ing's all a-bout. And

some kind of help is the kind of__ help we all can do with-out.

My brother's a pain.
He won't get out of bed
In the morning.
My mother has to carry him
Into the kitchen.
He opens his eyes
When he smells
His Sugar Pops.

He should get dressed
  himself.
He's six.
He's in first grade.
But he's so pokey
Daddy has to help him
Or he'd never be ready
  in time
And he'd miss the bus.

He cries if I
Leave without him.
Then Mom gets mad
And yells at me.
Which is another
  reason why
My brother's a pain.

He's got to be first
To show Mom
His school work.
She says *ooh* and *aah*
Over all his pictures.
Which aren't great at all
But just ordinary
First grade stuff.

At dinner he picks
At his food.
He's not supposed
To get dessert
If he doesn't
Eat his meat.
But he always
Gets it anyway.

When he takes a bath
My brother the pain
Powders the whole bathroom
And he never gets his face clean.
Daddy says
He's learning to
Take care of himself.
I say,
He's a slob!

Continued on page 64

The Great One

My sister thinks she's
  so great
Just because
  she's older.
Which makes Daddy
  and Mom think
She's really smart.
But I know the truth.
My sister's a jerk.

She thinks she's great
Just because she can
Play the piano.
And you can tell
The songs
  are real ones.
But I like
  my songs better.
Even if nobody
Ever heard them before.

My sister thinks she's so great
Just because she can work
The electric can opener.
Which means she gets
To feed the cat.
Which means the cat
Likes her better than me
Just because she feeds her.

My sister thinks she's so great
Just because Aunt Diana lets
Her watch the baby.
And tells her how much
The baby likes *her*.

And all the time
The baby is sleeping
In my dresser drawer.
Which my mother
  has fixed up
Like a bed
For when the baby
Comes to visit.

And I'm not supposed
To touch him
Even if he's
In *my* drawer
And gets changed
On *my* bed.

Continued on page 65

The Pain

My brother the pain
Is two years younger than me.
So how come
He gets to stay up
As late as I do?
Which isn't really late enough
For somebody in third grade
Anyway.

I asked Mom and
  Daddy about that.
They said,
"You're right.
You *are* older.
You *should* stay
  up later."

So they tucked the Pain
Into bed.
I couldn't wait
For the fun to begin.
I waited
And waited
And waited.
But Daddy and Mom
Just sat there
Reading books.

Finally I shouted,
"I'm going to bed!"

"We thought you wanted
To stay up later,"
They said.

"I did.
But without the Pain
There's nothing to do!"

"Remember that tomorrow,"
My mother said.
And she smiled.

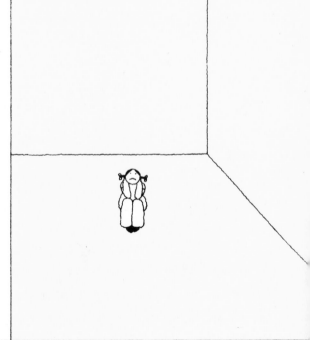

Continued on page 66

The Great One

My sister thinks she's so great
Just because she can
Remember phone numbers.
And when she dials
She never gets
The wrong person.

And when she has
  friends over
They build whole cities
Out of blocks.
I like to be garbage man.
I zoom my trucks
  all around.
So what if I
  knock down
Some of the buildings?

"It's not fair
That she always gets
To use
  the blocks!"
I told my mother
  and father.

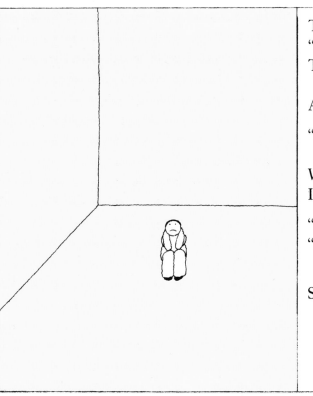

They said,
"You're right.
Today you can
  use the blocks
All by yourself."

"I'm going to build
  a whole city
Without you!"
I told the Great One.

"Go ahead," she said.
"Go build a whole
  state without me.

See if I care!"

So I did.
I built a whole
  country
All by myself.
Only it's not the
  funnest thing
To play blocks alone.
Because when I
  zoomed my trucks
And knocked down
  buildings
Nobody cared but me!

"Remember that tomorrow,"
Mom said, when I told her
I was through playing blocks.

Continued on page 67

The Pain

But the next day
My brother was
  a pain again.
When I got a phone call
He danced all around me
Singing stupid songs
At the top of his lungs.
Why does he have to
  act that way?

And why does he
  always
Want to be
  a garbage man
When I build a city
Out of blocks?
Who needs him
Knocking down
  buildings
With his dumb
  old trucks!

And I would really like to know
Why the cat sleeps on the Pain's bed
Instead of mine.
Especially since I am the one
Who feeds her.
That is the meanest thing of all!

I don't understand
How my mother can say
The Pain is lovable.
She's always kissing him
And hugging him
And doing disgusting things
Like that.
And my father says
The Pain is just what
They always wanted.

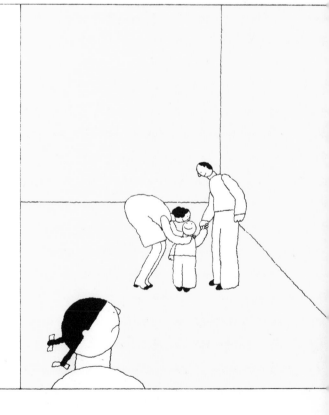

YUCK!

I think they love him better than me.

But the next day
We went swimming.
I can't stand my sister
When we go swimming.
She thinks she's so great
Just because she can
   swim and dive
And isn't afraid
To put her face
In the water.
I'm scared to
   put mine in
So she calls me *baby*.

Which is why
I have to
Spit water at her
And pull her hair
And even pinch her
Sometimes.

And I don't think it's fair
For Daddy and Mom to yell at me
Because none of it's my fault.
But they yell anyway.

Then my mother hugs my sister
And messes with her hair
And does other disgusting things
Like that.
And my father says
The Great One is just what
They always wanted.

YUCK!

I think they love her better than me.

Music by Stephen Lawrence   Lyrics by Bruce Hart

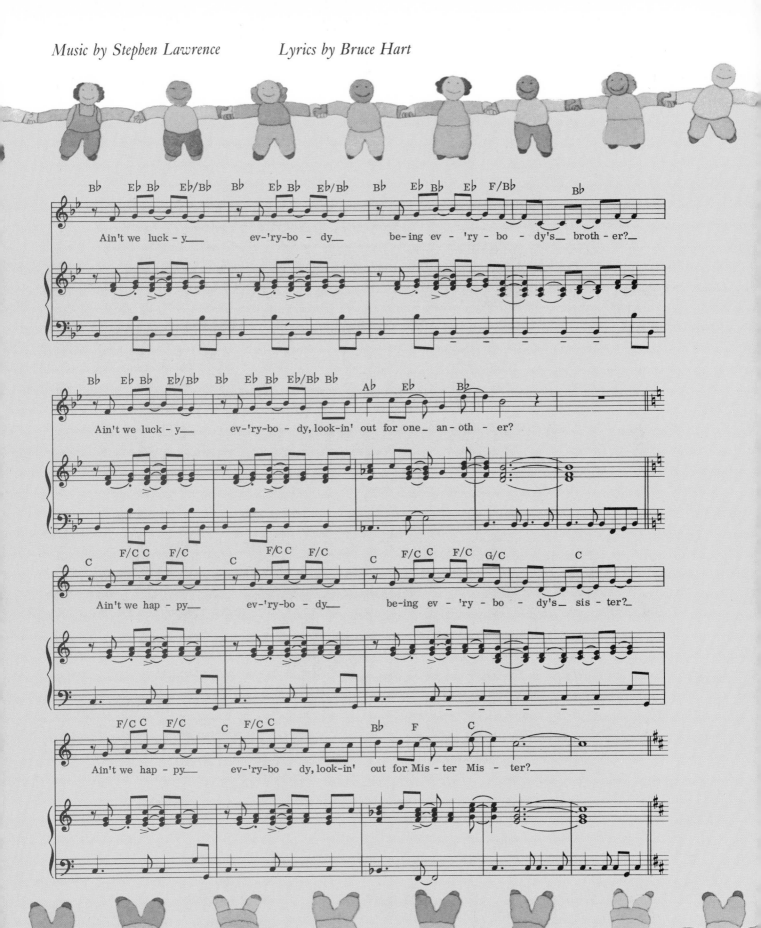

The Southpaw

by Judith Viorst

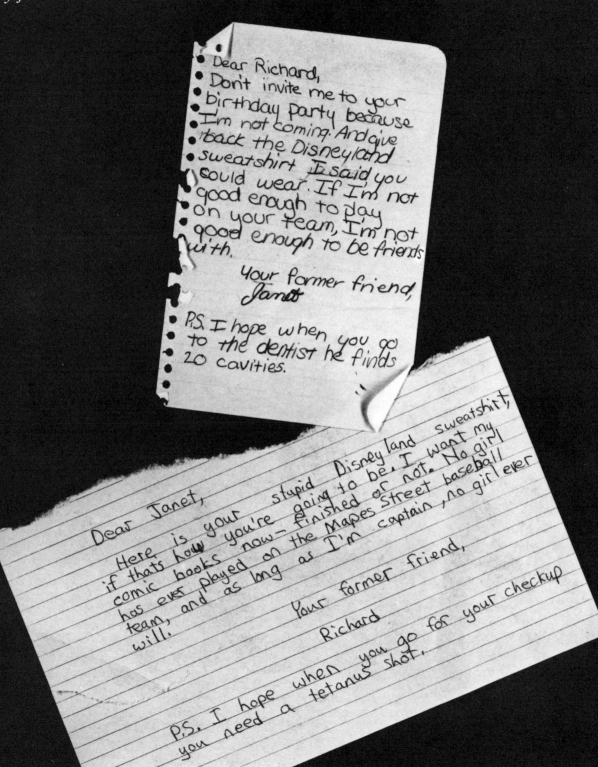

Dear Richard,
Don't invite me to your birthday party because I'm not coming. And give back the Disneyland sweatshirt I said you could wear. If I'm not good enough to play on your team, I'm not good enough to be friends with.

Your former friend,
Janet

P.S. I hope when you go to the dentist he finds 20 cavities.

Dear Janet,
Here is your stupid Disneyland sweatshirt, if thats how you're going to be. I want my comic books now — finished or not. No girl has ever played on the Mapes Street baseball team, and as long as I'm captain, no girl ever will.

Your former friend,
Richard

P.S. I hope when you go for your checkup you need a tetanus shot.

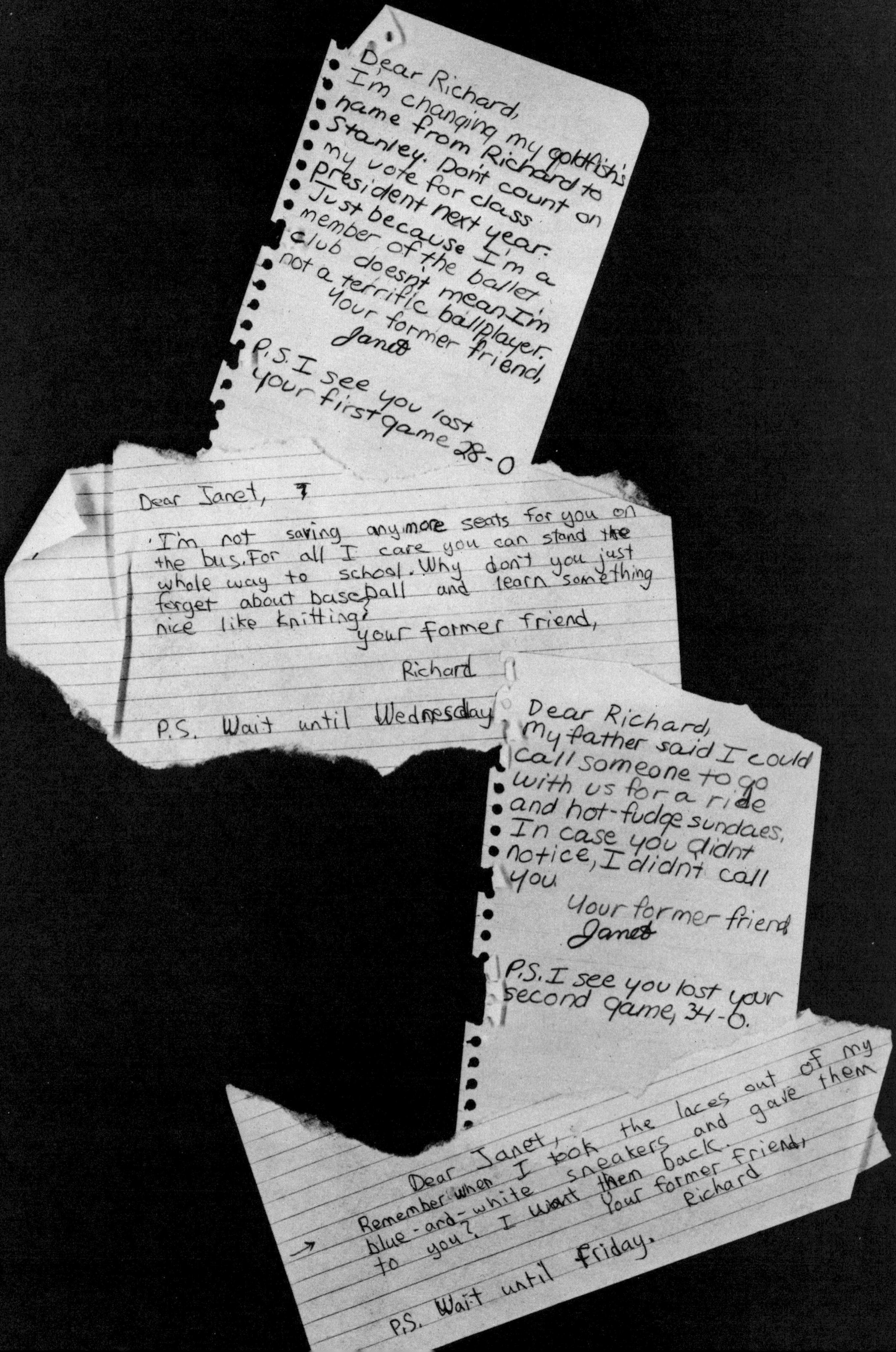

Dear Richard,
I'm changing my goldfish's
name from Richard to
Stanley. Don't count on
my vote for class
president next year.
Just because I'm a
member of the ballet
club doesn't mean I'm
not a terrific ballplayer.
Your former friend,
Janet

P.S. I see you lost
your first game 28-0

Dear Janet,

I'm not saving anymore seats for you on
the bus. For all I care you can stand the
whole way to school. Why don't you just
forget about baseball and learn something
nice like knitting?
Your former friend,

Richard

P.S. Wait until Wednesday.

Dear Richard,
My father said I could
call someone to go
with us for a ride
and hot-fudge sundaes.
In case you didn't
notice, I didn't call
you.
Your former friend,
Janet

P.S. I see you lost your
second game, 34-0.

Dear Janet, I took the laces out of my
Remember when I sneakers and gave them
blue-and-white back. I want them
to you? Your former friend,
Richard

P.S. Wait until Friday.

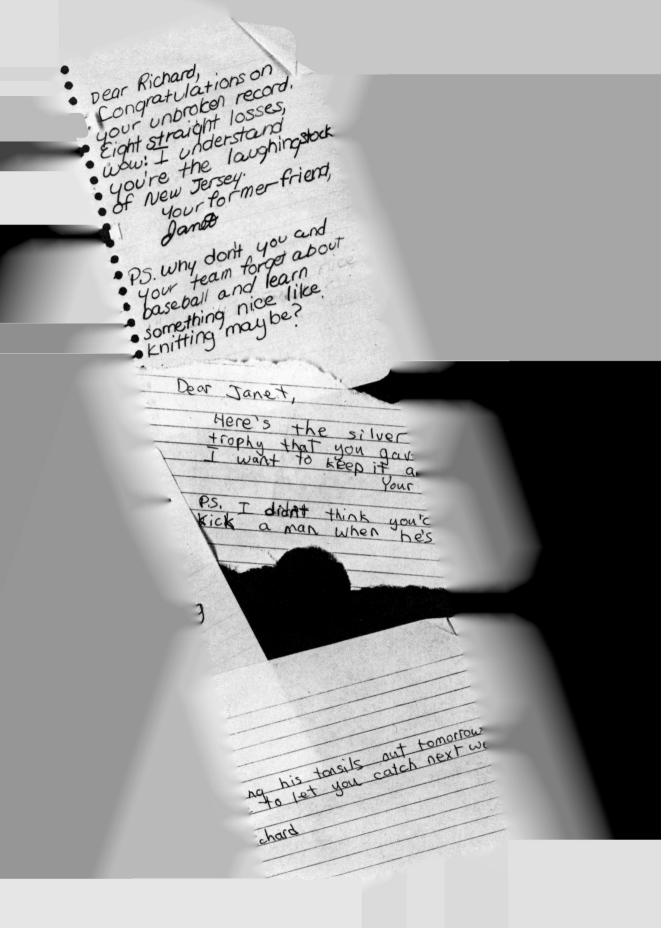

Dear Richard,
Congratulations on
your unbroken record.
Eight straight losses,
wow! I understand
you're the laughingstock
of New Jersey.
Your former-friend,
Janet

P.S. Why don't you and
your team forget about
baseball and learn
something nice like
knitting maybe?

Dear Janet,

Here's the silver
trophy that you gav
I want to keep it a
Your

P.S. I didn't think you'c
kick a man when he's

g

ng his tonsils out tomorrow
to let you catch next we

chard

Dear Richard,
I pitch.
     Janet

Dear Janet,
     Joel is moving to Kansas and Danny
sprained his wrist. How about a permanent
place in the outfield?
                    Richard

Dear Richard,
I pitch.
     Janet

Dear Janet,
     Ronnie caught the chicken pox and Leo
broke his toe and Elwood has these stupid
violin lessons. I'll give you first base,
and that's my final offer,
                    Richard

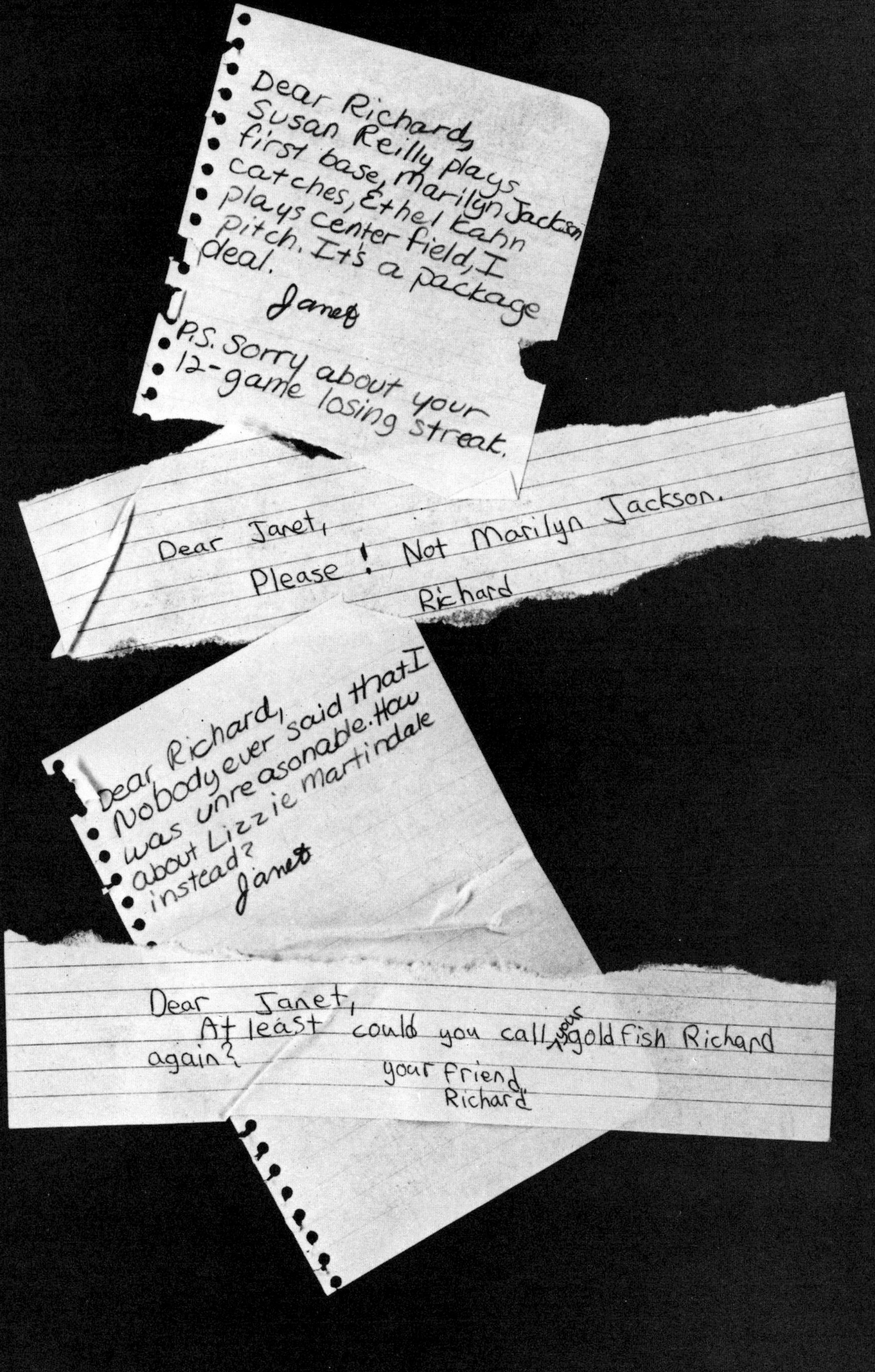

Dear Richard,
Susan Reilly plays
first base, Marilyn Jackson
catches, Ethel Kahn
plays center field, I
pitch. It's a package
deal.
        Janet

P.S. Sorry about your
12-game losing streak.

Dear Janet,
    Please! Not Marilyn Jackson.
                Richard

Dear Richard,
Nobody ever said that I
was unreasonable. How
about Lizzie Martindale
instead?
        Janet

Dear Janet,
    At least could you call your goldfish Richard
again?
                your friend,
                Richard

The Old Woman Who Lived in a Shoe

by Joyce Johnson

There was an old woman
   who lived in a shoe,
And all her grandchildren
   played there too.

She laughed at their jokes
   (when they were funny)
And kept a green jar
   of bubblegum money.
She rode with them
   on the carousel
And played Monopoly
   very well.

She taught them to paint
   and how to bake bread.
She read them riddles
   and tucked them in bed.
She taught them to sing
   and how to climb trees.
She patched their jeans
   and bandaged their knees.

She remembered the way
   she'd felt as a child,
The dreams she'd had
   of lands that were wild,
Of mountains to climb
   of villains to fight,
Of plays and poems
   she'd wanted to write.

She remembered all
   she'd wanted to do
Before she grew up
   and lived in the shoe.

There was an old woman
   who lived in a shoe
And lived in the dreams
   she'd had once too.
She told those she loved,
   "Children be bold.
Then you'll grow up
   But never grow old."

William's Doll

Music by Mary Rodgers
Lyric by Sheldon Harnick
Adapted from the book, William's Doll by Charlotte Zolotow

When my friend Wil-liam was five years old He wan-ted a doll to hug and hold. "A

doll," said Wil-liam, "is what I need to wash and clean and dress and feed; A doll to

give a bot-tle to And put to bed when day is through; And a-ny time my doll gets

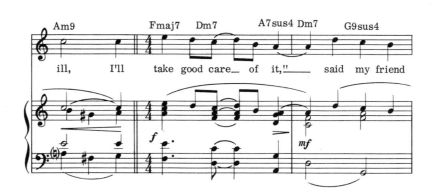

ill, I'll take good care of it," said my friend Bill.

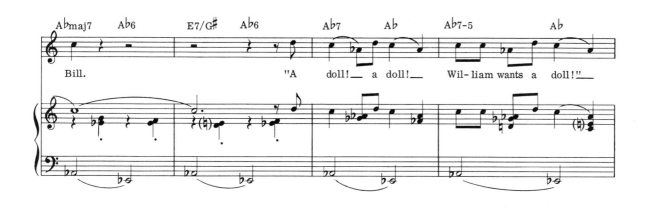

"A doll! a doll! Wil-liam wants a doll!"

"Don't be a sis-sy," said his best friend Ed. "Why should a boy want to play with a doll?"

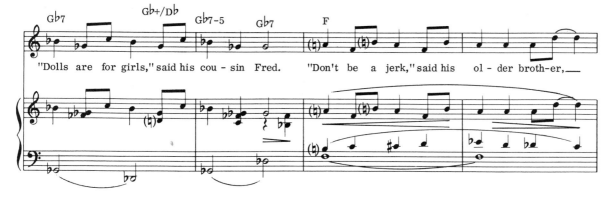

"Dolls are for girls," said his cou-sin Fred. "Don't be a jerk," said his ol-der broth-er,___

"I know what to do," said his fa-ther to his moth-er. So his

rit.

a tempo *mf*

fath - er bought him a bas - ket - ball, a bad-min-ton set___ and that's not all, A

bag of mar-bles, a base-ball glove and all the things___ a boy would love. And Bill was

good at ev - 'ry game, en-joyed them all but all___ the same when Bil - ly's

Bill said, "Base-ball's my fav-'rite game. I like to play, but

all the same, I'd give my bat and ball and glove to have a

doll that I could love." "How ve-ry wise," his grand-ma said. Said

Bill, "But ev-'ry one says this in-stead!: 'A

82

Waltz feeling

so when he has a ba-by some-day_____ he'll know how to dress it, put dia-pers on dou-ble, and gen-tly ca-ress it to bring up a bub-ble, and care for his ba-by as ev-'ry good

84

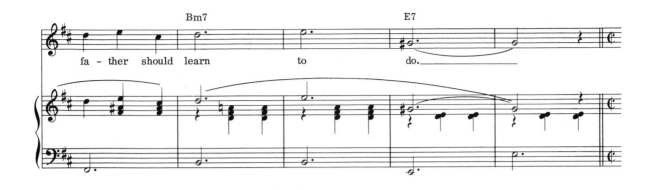

fa - ther should learn to do._____

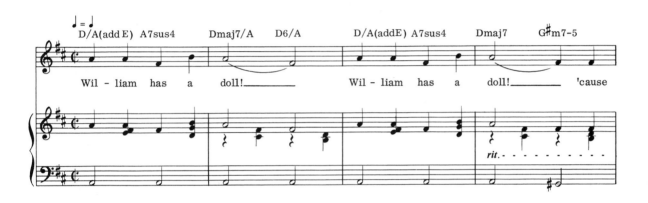

Wil - liam has a doll!_____ Wil - liam has a doll!_____ 'cause

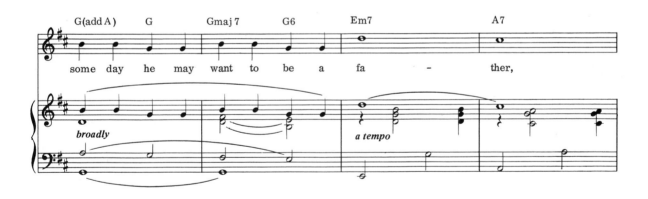

some day he may want to be a fa - ther,

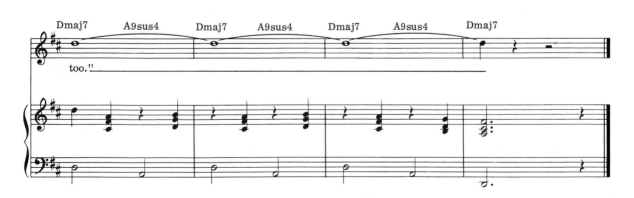

too."_____

85

My Dog Is a Plumber

by Dan Greenburg

My dog is a plumber, he must be a boy.
Although I must tell you his favorite toy
Is a little play stove with pans and with pots
Which he really must like, 'cause he plays with it lots.
So perhaps he's a girl, which kind of makes sense,
Since he can't throw a ball and he can't climb a fence.
But neither can Dad, and I know *he's* a man,
And Mom is a woman, and *she* drives a van.
Maybe the problem is in trying to tell
Just what someone is by what he does well.

Dudley Pippin and the Principal

by Phil Ressner

One day at school the sand table tipped over. Dudley Pippin's teacher thought Dudley had done it and she made him stay a long time after school. Dudley was very angry. On his way home he met the principal, who had a long nose and fierce eyes.

"Hello, Dudley," the principal said. "People are saying you tipped over the sand table at school today."

Dudley just shook his head, because he couldn't say anything. It wasn't fair.
The principal said, "Didn't you do it?"
Dudley shook his head.

"I *knew* you didn't do it," the principal said. "Your teacher must have made a mistake. It wasn't fair. We'll have to do something about it, first thing tomorrow morning."

Dudley nodded.
"I bet you'd like to cry," the principal said.

"No," Dudley said, and began to cry. "Boo-wah, hoo-wah," he cried. "Boo-hooh, wah-hoo, boo-hoo-wah." He cried a long time.

"That's fine," the principal said when Dudley was through.
"I'm sorry," Dudley said.
"What for?" the principal said. "You did that very well."
"But only sissies cry," Dudley said.

"A sissy," the principal said, "is somebody who *doesn't* cry because he's afraid people will call him a sissy if he *does.*"

"I'm all mixed up." Dudley said.

"Of course," the principal said. "Why should *you* be any different from everybody else? Most people spend their whole lives trying to get unmixed up."

Then he took a little blue flute out of his pocket. "Say," he said. "Just listen to this nice tune I learned yesterday; it's lovely."

And he began to play, and the music was sad and joyous and it filled the quiet street and went out over the darkling trees and the whole world.

It's All Right to Cry

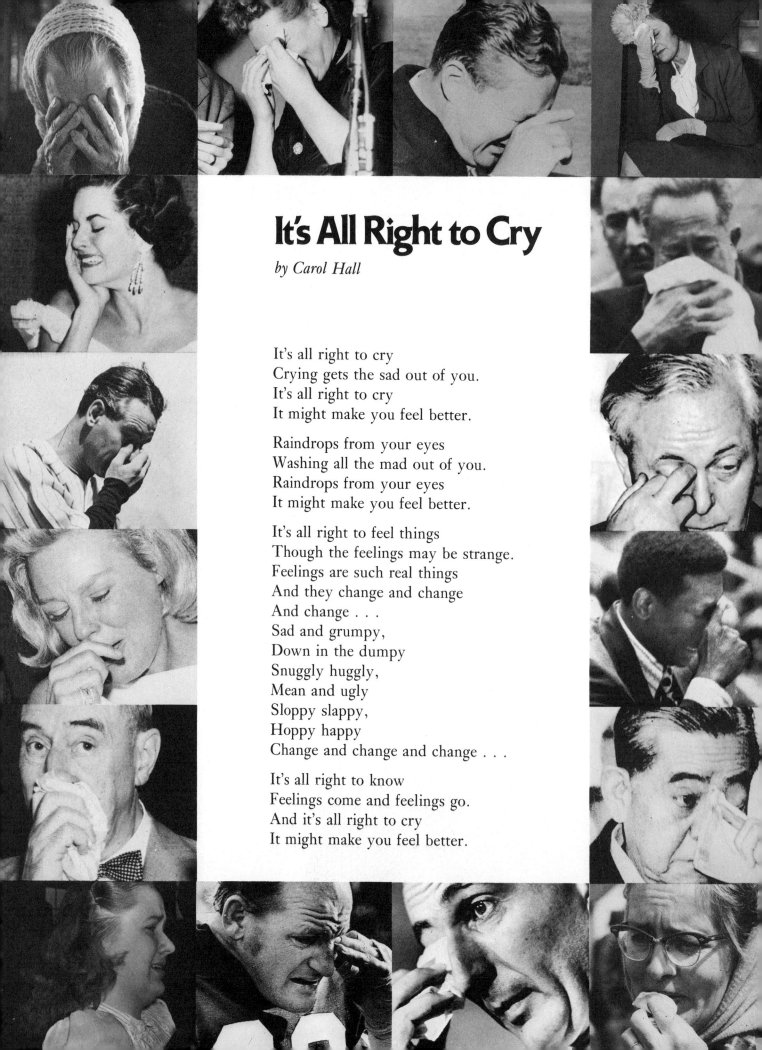

It's All Right to Cry

by Carol Hall

It's all right to cry
Crying gets the sad out of you.
It's all right to cry
It might make you feel better.

Raindrops from your eyes
Washing all the mad out of you.
Raindrops from your eyes
It might make you feel better.

It's all right to feel things
Though the feelings may be strange.
Feelings are such real things
And they change and change
And change . . .
Sad and grumpy,
Down in the dumpy
Snuggly huggly,
Mean and ugly
Sloppy slappy,
Hoppy happy
Change and change and change . . .

It's all right to know
Feelings come and feelings go.
And it's all right to cry
It might make you feel better.

It's All Right to Cry

It's all right to cry, Cry-ing gets the sad out of you. It's all right to
Rain-drops from your eyes, Wash-ing all the mad out of you. Rain-drops from your

cry, It might make you feel bet-ter.
eyes, It might make you feel bet-ter. It's all right to

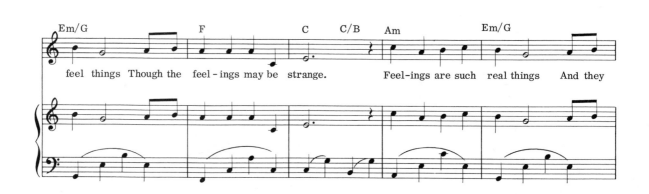

feel things Though the feel-ings may be strange. Feel-ings are such real things And they

The Field

by Anne Roiphe

Once there was a great field. At one edge of the field there were trees and bushes and on the other a thin country road that curved about untraveled for many miles.

In the field were rocks, high gray piles of stone, good for the climbing, hiding and exploring games of children.

In the middle of the field there was a tree, a single tree that had been growing for more than a hundred years. It was gnarled and its branches spread in many directions. The children from the neighboring villages would use the tree for home base in their games of tag and hide-and-go-seek.

The field lay just between the Kingdoms of Aura and Ghent. Both kings claimed the field even though it was bare except for the rocks and the tree and the children who played in it.

"Mine," said the King of Aura, politely.

"Mine," answered the King of Ghent in a louder voice.

Then the people of both countries began to say ugly things about each other.

And soon two armies gathered—one on each side of the field.

The battle began. The Aurians were camped by the bushes and the trees and the Ghentians were over on the other side of the road.

In the tree in the middle of the field a robin had built her nest of twigs and grass. She had woven it together and now the nest hidden by the summer leaves held three blue eggs. Carefully, the mother sat on her eggs even though the arrows whizzed past the tree and the shotguns made sounds of thunder and there was the sound of screaming when soldiers were hurt or frightened. The bird stayed on her nest although there was crying and singing and shouting as the men moved up to the foot of the tree and then retreated.

One morning when the soldiers were starting to shoot at each other again, the robin flew down to the grass and unearthed a worm. As she pulled it from the soil, the guns pounded the ground and the soldiers moved up and down, hiding and crawling in the thick grass, and there was smoke in the air and blood on the rocks where the children had played.

As the robin was flying back to her nest an arrow with a sharp tip flew past the

97

crouching soldiers and pierced the throat of the bird. Her wings fluttered for a moment and then she fell like a heavy stone. Only one soldier saw her fall.

Then a shell from the king's prize cannon boomed across the field and landed not far from the tree.

The earth shook and the tree trembled and the branches wavered and the nest with the three small eggs fell down to the ground.

The young soldier watched the nest fall. He crawled over the rocks and the twigs and found the three small eggs unbroken. Not even a crack was on the shells.

The soldier put his shotgun down on the ground. He took off his iron gray helmet, and turning it over, he filled it with grass and a dandelion and some clover. He carefully placed the nest in the matted grass and cradled the helmet in his arms. He sat for awhile watching the eggs in his helmet.

The commanding officer came by and saw one of his soldiers sitting down.

"Come on soldier, let's go . . . put your helmet on."

The young man, carrying his helmet, reached for his gun and started forward.

"Put your helmet on," the officer shouted.

There was a pause as the soldier looked down at the eggs.

"I can't sir," he said.

"There's no such thing as can't in this man's army," yelled the officer. "Put your helmet on your head."

The soldier put down his gun.

"I think," he said in a very quiet voice, "I think I'm going home now sir."

The commanding officer turned red in the face but the young man, carefully holding his helmet under his arm, turned around and walked off the field, past the bushes and trees.

On his way home the three eggs broke open and three small wet birds opened their tiny beaks for food. The soldier stopped. He gathered some berries from a nearby bush and offered them gently to each bird in turn. The soldier smiled. Then the birds settled down, resting on one another, and fell asleep.

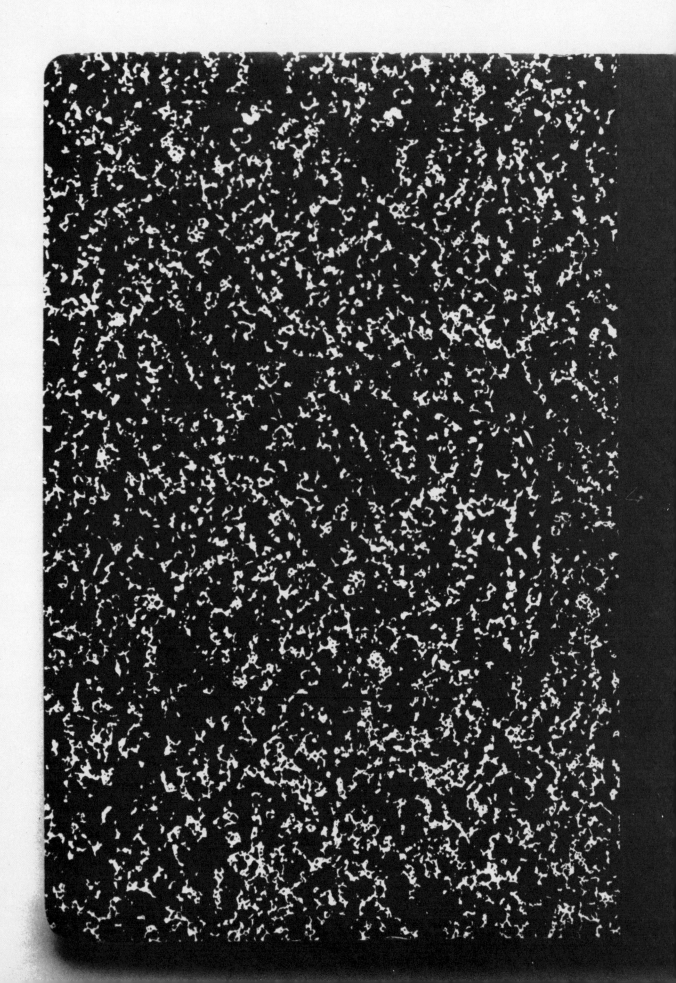

by Herb Gardner

How I Crossed the Street for the First Time All by Myself

JULES SIEGLE-Class 4A
Miss Gresham, Composition Class
P. S. 92, Brooklyn, New York

First of all this composition is about how I crossed the street all by myself for the first time which was when I was around five years old which was four years ago when I was a kid. First of all when I was around five every time I even just lightly put my foot down in the gutter for a second my Mother would say Jules you go off the sidewalk and you're going to get it. That means when I'm going to get it it means I'm going to get hit. Usually most of the time when she says I'm going to get it she doesn't really mean it she's going to hit me and she can't hit very hard anyway it means something I'm not going to get like ice cream.

When my Mother says like that Jules you're going to get it she says it like this, JueWOOLS, with the WOOLS part louder and it could fool you her voice I mean because you'd think it was the loudest voice in the whole world when really it's not loud it's the way she says it scary and sharp like in a movie I saw when John Wayne he says to this bad guy low and scary and you could tell he hated him and it was like my Mother says what she says. My Mother is nice when she doesn't yell. But she yells a lot.

Now I'll tell you about the part about when I crossed the street for the first time by myself. When I was around that age, a lot of times and even now it still happens a funny thing when I learn a new word. See I'll hear a word for the first time like yesterday I heard this word drainage and when I heard it I was in JACK'S having a chocolate malted and I was looking over at the Boston Cream Pie they got covered up with a plastic cover and now every time I hear that word or even think of that word I get this picture in my mind of this Boston Cream Pie with a plastic cover over it. They got nothing to do with each other, Boston Cream Pie and this word drainage, but the thing is that's how it works out I get this picture in my mind. Well this doesn't happen much now but boy when I was five years old I was learning a lot of new words and that thing with the picture in my mind would happen all the time. One time when I was five I learned six new words right in front of a big green garage on Bedford Avenue. Well these were extremely used a lot words and I kept getting this picture in my mind of this garage, the green one. So the thing is I told my Mother about it not because it bothered me or anything but because I thought it was a pretty interesting thing and she didn't listen and the thing was I started to cry because she wasn't paying attention.

I cry easy, not anymore, I mean when I was five. Well boy she got annoyed about me crying because of nothing and I just kept right up this crying for five minutes around and telling her about this garage thing again and then she got real angry, I mean boy she was extremely angry and she said this thing, she said, stop crying, you look ugly when you cry, like a little rat. The thing is when you get down to it I wasn't a very good looking kid.

My brother is the kind of little kid you get excited about, I mean he's a really good looking kid, Jerry. His hair is blond and he looks like once I saw on the Saturday Evening Post which we have a subscription to that comes every week. I like the cartoons pretty much. My brother he was three when I was five I mean he really knocks your eye out. My grandmother every time she saw him she'd have a fit right there on the street. And she'd keep saying Shaneh Yingle which is Jewish words for a really good looking kid. Right on the street she'd have a fit. Nobody much said anything to me like that except my Uncle Herschel who said I was intelligent once when we were having a picnic the whole family out in the park.

It didn't bother me right away about me being a little rat because I didn't even know what a rat was at that time being young like I was. So I asked Lester who was always breaking his arm. This boy Lester was older than me at that time and he was about ten years old which is what I am now practically and he was always breaking his ankle or his wrist or his arm. He roller skated a lot and I think that's how it always happened with him running into a truck. And he had one operation when they took out his whole appendix that left a scar that he'll show you if you ask him and sometimes even if you don't.

So I came up to Lester and his arm was in a cast from his hand up past his elbow and I wanted to speak to him personal so I waited till a time when there was not a lot of kids around which is not extremely often because he has a lot of friends, arms over each others shoulders when you walk down the street kind of friends. I don't have friends much especially that kind at that time. Not like put their arms around your shoulders when you walk down the street. Sometimes kids would want to do like that with me but I cut it out because I knew they didn't really mean it because when you get right down to it they didn't like me. The thing was I cried a lot at that time and they heard me I'm pretty sure because we were all together living altogether in the same apartment house and the thing was I cried extremely. And they all could do things like one kid was a good climber, like on fences and things and I didn't do anything much and I still had to wear my blue snowsuit from when I was four and other kids was wearing longies in the winter and a snowsuit like I had it's all made from one big piece so when say you bend your elbow, you can feel it pulling at your ankle. And my Mother didn't let me cross the street by myself yet. So I went up to Lester and he had this cast on his arm and all his friends what could write they signed names with an ink pen on the dirty white cast, a lot of friends, names all over, friends crowded all the way up to his elbow.

said to Lester I said what is a rat Lester so he said to me Jules a rat is like Mickey Mouse only different so I said like Mickey Mouse only different, well how much different is that Lester I said so he said before he told me anymore we had to play a game of who can hit the lightest which is a silly game that was a joke that Lester always pulled where he'd say to a kid let's see who can hit the lightest and you'd go first and give him a real light marshmallo tap on the shoulder and then he'd say now it was his turn and he'd give you a real big smash in the arm that would hurt you like your arm was coming off and then Lester would shout out he lost and then he'd laugh like his head was going to fall off. So he played that a little while till it got dull. So then he said you want to see what a rat is so I said yeah so he said O.K., I'll show you so he took me down in his basement of his house where he lived and there was this little hole in the wall near the floor and we sat there in the dark for a long time and then this little thing came out and Lester said Jules that's a rat. It made me cry extremely to see what it was, a rat.

ext morning when I woke up the first thing I heard was the High Cash Clothes Man down in the front of the apartment house. Highcashclothes he was yelling like always. He's a man like they got men like that who go around in the morning around the neighborhood yelling up at the apartments Highcashclothes and he's got this bundle of clothes and raggy stuff over his back and he's pretty old, older than Lester and my mother and even my grandmother, and the ladies in the apartment house they sometimes some of them would open up their window and say to him he should come upstairs and they give him the number where they lived and then he'd come up and real cheap he'd buy clothes and shoes off them and later he would sell all the clothes and make some money himself, but most of the time nobody opened up the window and he'd just keep yelling and then he'd keep quiet maybe he'd hear a window open he'd just stop and listen for a while but he didn't hear nothing so then he'd go away to the next house yelling only sometimes it was like he was singing and he didn't have any hair and he was very old.

So that morning when I heard him I figured I would run away with him and help him because his voice was getting tired and one thing I could do I could sure yell loud and I could do the yelling part of the job and we would go all around is what I thought at that time so I went down in the street and I said to him what I thought about how I would yell for him and all so you know what he said the thing he said was he didn't need nobody and he said thank you anyway and he was real nice about it and he smiled and then he gave me a scarf from the stuff he had. It was a very nice scarf except it had holes. I told him if I practiced up the yelling part maybe next year, anyway he said I couldn't and then he went away.

So he went away and I was just standing there on the street by myself and I got this feeling soon I got to cross the street that day maybe and I got this terrible feeling to do something because Lester broke his arm and knew things and the other kids they climbed or something and one kid could sound like different kinds of birds and my Mother she told me once that when I was little and all the babies said bye bye in their carriages and did tricks I didn't do anything she says I just sat in my carriage and stared like I was sick. But when I was five all the kids my age none of them were allowed to cross the street themselves without anybody and they had to go over to an old man and say Mister will you cross me, so it came to me I should cross the street and not just a thin little street like going to the other side of my block but a extremely big street like on the corner, Flatbush Avenue.

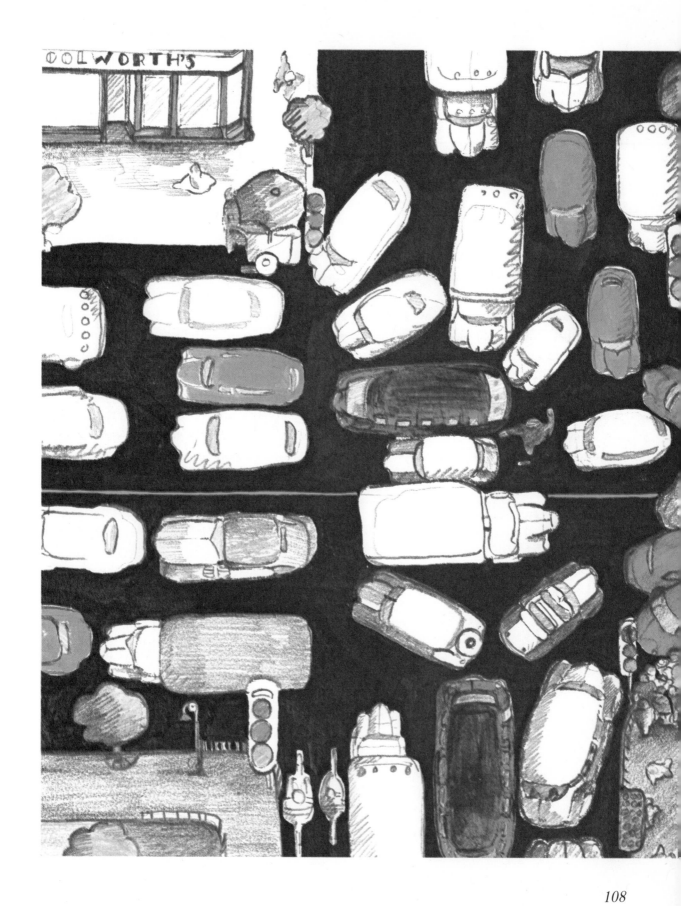

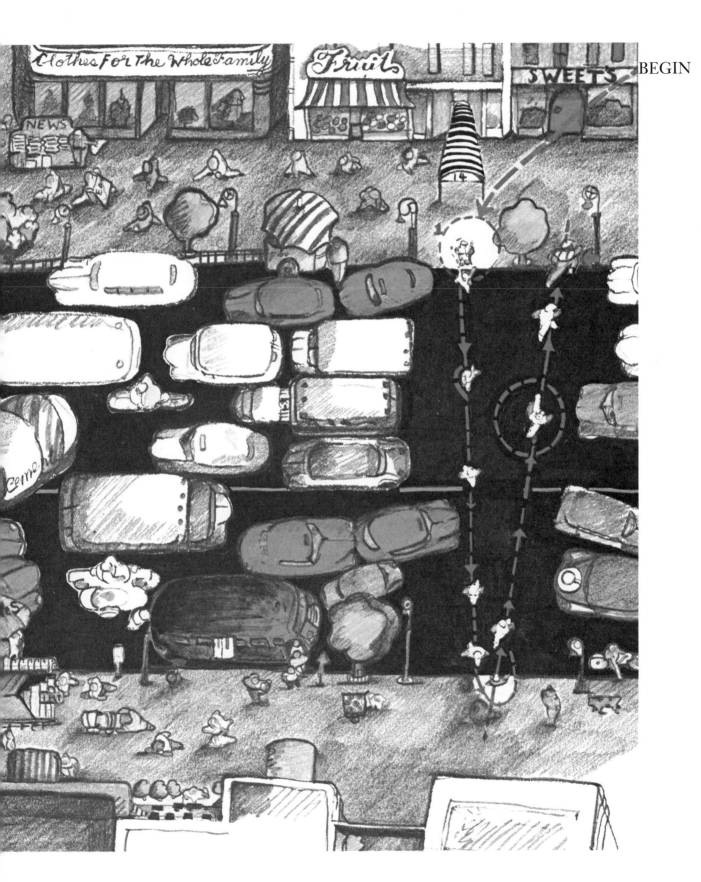

BEGIN

109

So then I heard my Mother from upstairs in the apartment she started to call JueWOOLS LUNCH JueWOOLS JueWOOLS and I was just standing around figuring about crossing Flatbush because I didn't want to do it right away because I was scared and she kept going JueWOOLS JueWOOLS LUNCH so I started for the corner which was a little way up the block because our apartment house where we live was in the middle of the block and she kept calling JueWOOLS like I told you she does.

When I got to the corner I was very scared because of all the cars and all the trucks and all the trolleys and everything was very big and moving and the other side of the avenue it looked so far away. My apartment house was pretty far away down the block but I could still hear my mother with the corner of my ear and she was going JueWOOLS JueWOOLS and then she stopped going like that and I couldn't hear her and I figured she must be coming to get me so I had to cross then because I had to, so two fists I made and I closed my eyes shut tight 'till it hurt a little in my head and then I bent my head over and then I ran.

It didn't feel good while I was running because it was like a coward and with my head all bent down scared and it was all twitchy and small like the thing that come out of the hole in Lester's basement and I knew I was on the other side because all of a sudden I tripped over the curb.

I opened my eyes up and I looked across Flatbush where I ranned from and across Flatbush and down my block I could see my Mother coming out of our apartment house and I felt bad because she didn't see me cross for myself so then she started to come where I was and she was too far away for me to see her face good but just how she walked I could see she was angry and I was going to get it.

It was really a good time to cry but the thing was I didn't cry. I just kept thinking that I wanted to cross back to her by myself and show her before she could get across and bring me back. I knew I was going to get it but I didn't think about that and I didn't cry and she was getting close to the corner on the other side and I had to do it soon and I could see her face now clearer and she was so angry she was crying but the thing was I wasn't crying and I came back across the street to her not like before, eyes closed and bent over like the thing from the hole but I came back slow, like marching, like how they march in a parade.

No One Else

by Elaine Laron
drawings by Daniel Pinchbeck, age 7

Now, someone else can tell you how
To multiply by three
And someone else can tell you how
To spell Schenectady
And someone else can tell you how
To ride a two-wheeled bike
But no one else, no, no one else
Can tell you what to like.

An engineer can tell you how
To run a railroad train
A map can tell you where to find
The capital of Spain
A book can tell you all the names
Of every star above
But no one else, no, no one else
Can tell you who to love.

Your aunt Louise can tell you how
To plant a pumpkin seed
Your cousin Frank can tell you how
To catch a centipede
Your Mom and Dad can tell you how
To brush between each meal
But no one else, no, no one else
Can tell you how to feel.

For how you feel is how you feel
And all the whole world through
No one else, no, no one else
Knows *that* as well as YOU!

Three Wishes

by Lucille Clifton

Everybody knows there's such a thing as luck. Like when a good man be the first person to come in your house on the New Year Day you have a good year, but I know somethin better than that! Find a penny on the New Year Day with your birthday on it, and you can make three wishes on it and the wishes will come true! It happened to me.

First wish was when I found the penny. Me and Victorius Richardson was goin for a walk, wearin our new boots we got for Christmas and our new hat and scarf sets when I saw somethin all shiny in the snow.

Victor say, "What is that, Lena?"

"Look like some money," I say, and I picked it up. It was a penny with my birthday on it. 1962.

Victor say, "Look like you in for some luck now, Lena. That's a lucky penny for you. What you gonna wish?"

"Well, one thing I do wish is it wasn't so cold," I say just halfway jokin. And the sun come out. Just then.

Well, that got me thinkin. Me and Victor started back to my house both of us thinkin bout the penny and what if there really is such a thing and what to wish in case. Mama was right in the living room when we got to the house.

"How was the walk, Nobie?"

"Fine thank you, Mama," I say.

"Fine thank you, ma'am," Victor say as we went back to the kitchen.

My name is Zenobia after somebody in the Bible. My name is Zenobia and everybody calls me Nobie. Everybody but Victor. He calls me Lena after Lena Horne and when I get grown I'm goin to Hollywood and sing in the movies and Victorius is gonna go with me 'cause he my best friend. That's his real name.

Back in the kitchen it was nice and warm 'cause the stove was lit and Mama had opened the oven door. Me and Victor sat at the table talkin soft so nobody would hear.

"You get two more wishes, Lena."

"You really think there's somethin to it?"

"What you mean, didn't you see how the sun come ridin out soon as you said about it bein too cold?"

"You really think so?"

"Man, don't you believe nothin?"

"I just don't believe everything like you do, that's all!"

"Well, you just simple!"

"Who you callin simple?"

"Simple you, that's who, simple Zenobia!"

I jumped up from the table, "Man, I wish you would get out of here!" and Victor jumped up and ran out of the room and grabbed his coat and ran out of the house. Just then.

Well, I'm tellin you! I just sat back down at the table and shook my head. I had just about wasted another wish! I didn't have but one more left!

Mama came into the kitchen lookin for me. "Zenobia, what was the matter with Victorius?" She call me Zenobia when she kind of mad.

"We was just playin, Mama."

"Well, why did he run out of here like that?"

"I don't know Mama, that's how Victor is."

"Well, I hope you wasn't bein unfriendly to him Zenobia, 'cause I know how you are too."

"Yes, ma'am. Mama, what would you wish for if you could have anything you wanted in the whole wide world?"

Mama sat down at the table and started playin with the salt shaker. "What you mean, Nobie?"

"I mean, if you could have yourself one wish, what would it be for?"

Mama put the salt back on a straight line with the pepper and got the look on her face like when she tellin me the old wise stuff.

"Good friends, Nobie. That's what we need in this world. Good friends." Then she went back to playin with the table.

Well, I didn't think she was gonna say that! Usually when I hear the grown people talkin bout different things they want, they be talkin bout money or a good car or somethin like that. Mama always do come up with a surprise!

I got up and got my coat and went to sit out on the step. I started thinkin bout ole Victor and all the stuff me and him used to do. Goin to the movies and practicin my singin and playin touch ball and stick ball and one time we found a rock with a whole lotta shiny stuff in it look just like a diamond. One time me and him painted a picture of the whole school. He was really a good friend to me. Never told one of my secrets. Hard to find friends like that.

"Wish I still had a good friend," I whispered to myself, holdin the penny real tight and feelin all sorry for myself.

And who do you think come bustin down the street grinnin at me? Just then!

Yeah, there's such a thing as luck. Lot of people think they know different kinds of luck but this thing bout the penny is really real. I know 'cause just like I say, it happened to me.

Glad to Have a Friend Like You

by Carol Hall

Jill told Bill
That it was lots of fun to cook.
Bill told Jill
That she could bait a real fish hook.

    So they made ooey gooey
    Chocolate cake
    Sticky licky
    Sugar top
    And they gobbled it and giggled.
    And they sat by the river
    And they fished in the water
    And they talked
    As the squirmy wormies wiggled,
    Singin'

    Glad to have a friend like you,
    Fair and fun and skippin' free.
    Glad to have a friend like you,
    And glad to just be me.

Pearl told Earl
That they could do a secret code.
Earl told Pearl
There was free ice cream when it snowed.

    So they sent funny letters
    Which contained mystery messages
    And nobody knew just how they made it.

    And they raised up the window
    And they scooped all the snow together,
    Put milk and sugar in and ate it,
    Singin'

    Glad to have a friend like you,
    Fair and fun and skippin' free.
    Glad to have a friend like you,
    And glad to just be me.

Peg told Greg
She liked to make things out of chairs.
Greg told Peg
Sometimes he still hugged teddy bears.

    So they sneaked in the living room
    And piled all the pillows up
    And made it a rocket ship
    To fly in.
    And the bears were their girls and boys
    And they were the astronauts
    Who lived on the moon
    With one pet lion,
    Singin'

    Glad to have a friend like you,
    Fair and fun and skippin' free.
    Glad to have a friend like you,
    And glad to just be me.

Glad to Have a Friend Like You

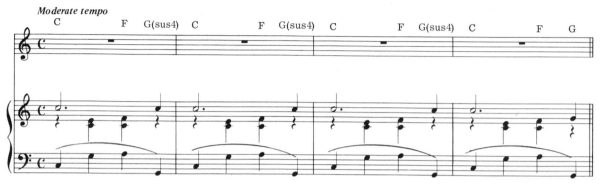

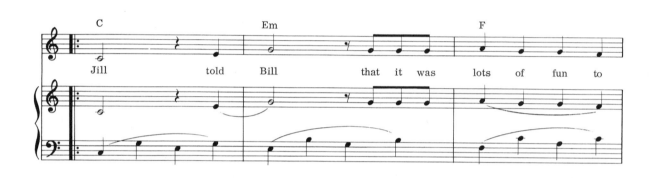

Jill told Bill that it was lots of fun to

cook. Bill told Jill that she could bait a real fish -

hook.

So they made oo - ey goo - ey choc - olate cake stick - y lick - y sug - ar top and they gob - bled it and gig - gled.__ And they sat by the riv - er and they fished in the wa - ter and they

talked as the squirm-y worm-ies wig-gled,_ Sing-in' Glad to have a

friend like you, fair, and fun, and skip-pin' free.

Glad to have a friend like you, and glad to just be me.

Glad to just be, glad to just be me. Glad to just be, glad to just be me.

Fine

Zachary's Divorce

by Linda Sitea

On this particular Saturday morning Zachary's toes woke up first. They wiggled and wiggled and wiggled in the warm sunlight streaming through the windows. Zachary could feel them wiggling but he couldn't see them because his eyes were still asleep. Next, his arms and mouth woke up and together gave a gigantic stretch and yawn. The yawn sounded something like this: "Aaarrr." Then his whole body woke up and turned over and over, quickly, and before the last turn was done his eyes opened and Zachary was all awake.

Slowly he climbed out of bed and tiptoed across the rug. He moved carefully, so he wouldn't step on the blue and green flowers, only the purple ones, because purple was his favorite color.

He went straight to Mommy's and Daddy's room. He looked at Mommy sleeping in Mommy's and Daddy's bed. He looked at the wood sculptures he had made in school that were nailed into the wall. He looked at the leafy avocado plant that was almost to the ceiling, just the right size for pretending you were an explorer lost in the jungle. Zachary looked at the bookshelves and the easel and Mommy's paintings. He even looked in the closets and under the bed. Daddy was not there.

Next he went into the bathroom. And while he was there he sang a little song:

La la pee dee
La la pee vee
La la pee gee

Daddy was not in the bathroom.

Zachary slid down the stairs on his stomach, bump bump, bump.

He walked back and forth from the living room to the dining room four times and tried to practice his whistling. But no whistle came out, only a puff of wind.

Zachary looked at the bookshelves and his favorite plant that was all purple.

Daddy wasn't in the living room either.

Next Zachary went into the kitchen and there on the wall was his best invention. He turned the handle and the pulley went around and the rope pulled the refrigerator door open. Daddy had helped him build it but it was all his own idea. Daddy and Mommy had said it was a really great idea because you could open the refrigerator door without walking all the way over to it. Zachary closed the door now. He didn't feel like any orange juice this morning. No Daddy in the kitchen.

124

Zachary went back into the living room and sat on the big chair. He pulled Mommy's patchwork quilt over him and settled in. It was usually a very happy patchwork quilt with every color you could think of in it. But it didn't seem so happy lately.

The morning is a very sad time if you have a divorce, Zachary thought. Having a divorce meant that you woke up in the morning and your Daddy was not there because now Daddy lived in another house. Then Zachary thought of Amy who was in school with him. And he remembered how Amy's divorce meant that she woke up in the morning and her Daddy was there but not her Mommy. He wondered how grown-ups decided which kind of divorce to give you, the Mommy kind or the Daddy kind. Then he tried to figure out, if he could choose, which he would rather have, the Mommy kind or the Daddy kind. But it gave him a headache just to think about it.

Zachary stared out the window. "The morning is a very sad time when you have a divorce," Zachary said out loud.

"I know how you feel. Sometimes the morning is very sad for me too," said Mommy, standing on the bottom step. Mommy was wearing her blue T-shirt and the dungarees Zachary liked best of all—the ones with the bright purple paint on them.

Mommy came and cuddled into the big chair with Zachary and pulled the patchwork quilt over her too.

Zachary whispered, "Mommy tell me the story again about why I got a divorce."

Mommy hugged Zachary very hard and then said: "It's not your divorce Zachary, it's Daddy's and mine. We decided we would be happier if we lived apart from each other. You mustn't think it's because of anything you did wrong, because it isn't. Daddy and I have always loved you very much and always will. And remember, you see Daddy a lot and sleep over at his house a lot too."

Zachary snuggled closer to Mommy.

"Do you think Daddy is sometimes sad in the morning too?" Zachary asked.

"Yes, I think he is," said Mommy. "It's okay to be sad. This is a very new thing that has happened to us. But really, as time passes, we'll all get used to the divorce and we'll be less and less and less sad."

"Let's go get some orange juice," Zachary shouted, and ran into the kitchen.

As he turned the pulley handle to open the refrigerator, Zachary pretended time was passing with each turn. And with each turn, he told himself that soon he would feel less and less and less sad.

Atalanta

by Betty Miles

Once upon a time, not long ago, there lived a princess named Atalanta, who could run as fast as the wind.

She was so bright, and so clever, and could build things and fix things so wonderfully, that many young men wished to marry her.

"What shall I do?" said Atalanta's father, who was a powerful king. "So many young men want to marry you, and I don't know how to choose."

"You don't have to choose, Father," Atalanta said. "I will choose. And I'm not sure that I will choose to marry anyone at all."

"Of course you will," said the king. "Everybody gets married. It is what people do."

"But," Atalanta told him, with a toss of her head, "I intend to go out and see the world. When I come home, perhaps I will marry and perhaps I will not."

The king did not like this at all. He was a very ordinary king; that is, he was powerful and used to having his own way. So he did not answer Atalanta, but simply told her, "I have decided how to choose the young man you will marry. I will hold a great race, and the winner—the swiftest, fleetest young man of all—will win the right to marry you."

Now Atalanta was a clever girl as well as a swift runner. She saw that she might win both the argument and the race—provided that she herself could run in the race, too. "Very well," she said. "But you must let me race along with the others. If I am

129

not the winner, I will accept the wishes of the young man who is."

The king agreed to this. He was pleased; he would have his way, marry off his daughter, and enjoy a fine day of racing as well. So he directed his messengers to travel throughout the kingdom announcing the race with its wonderful prize: the chance to marry the bright Atalanta.

As the day of the race drew near, flags were raised in the streets of the town, and banners were hung near the grassy field where the race would be run. Baskets of ripe plums and peaches, wheels of cheese, ropes of sausages and onions, and loaves of crusty bread were gathered for the crowds.

Meanwhile, Atalanta herself was preparing for the race. Each day at dawn, dressed in soft green trousers and a shirt of yellow silk, she went to the field in secret and ran across it—slowly at first, then fast and faster, until she could run the course more quickly than anyone had ever run it before.

As the day of the race grew nearer, young men began to crowd into the town. Each was sure he could win the prize, except for one; that was Young John, who lived in the town. He saw Atalanta day by day as she bought nails and wood to make a pigeon house, or chose parts for her telescope, or laughed with her friends. Young John saw the princess only from a distance, but near enough to know how bright and clever she was. He wished very much to race with her, to win, and to earn the right to talk with her and become her friend.

"For surely," he said to himself, "it is not right for Atalanta's father to give her away to the winner of the race. Atalanta herself must choose the person she wants to marry, or whether she wishes to marry at all. Still, if I could only win the race, I would be free to speak to her, and to ask for her friendship."

Each evening, after his studies of the stars and the seas, Young John went to the field in secret and practiced running across it. Night after night, he ran fast as the wind across the twilight field, until he could cross it more quickly than anyone had every crossed it before.

At last, the day of the race arrived.

Trumpets sounded in the early morning, and the young men gathered at the edge of the field, along with Atalanta herself, the prize they sought. The king and his friends sat in soft chairs, and the townspeople stood along the course.

The king rose to address them all. "Good day," he said to the crowds. "Good luck," he said to the young men. To Atalanta he said, "Good-bye. I must tell you farewell, for tomorrow you will be married."

"I am not so sure of that, Father," Atalanta answered. She was dressed for the race in trousers of crimson and a shirt of silk as blue as the sky, and she laughed as she looked up and down the line of young men.

"Not one of them," she said to herself, "can win the race, for I will run fast as the wind and leave them all behind."

And now a bugle sounded, a flag was dropped, and the runners were off!

133

The crowds cheered as the young men and Atalanta began to race across the field. At first they ran as a group, but Atalanta soon pulled ahead, with three of the young men close after her. As they neared the halfway point, one young man put on a great burst of speed and seemed to pull ahead for an instant, but then he gasped and fell back. Atalanta shot on.

Soon another young man, tense with the effort, drew near to Atalanta. He reached out as though to touch her sleeve, stumbled for an instant, and lost speed. Atalanta smiled as she ran on. I have almost won, she thought.

But then another young man came near. This was Young John, running like the wind, as steadily and as swiftly as Atalanta herself. Atalanta felt his closeness, and in a sudden burst she dashed ahead.

Young John might have given up at this, but he never stopped running. Nothing at all, thought he, will keep me from winning the chance to speak with Atalanta. And on he ran, swift as the wind, until he ran as her equal, side by side with her, toward the golden ribbon that marked the race's end. Atalanta raced even faster to pull ahead, but Young John was a strong match for her. Smiling with the pleasure of the race, Atalanta and Young John reached the finish line together, and together they broke through the golden ribbon.

Trumpets blew. The crowd shouted and leaped about. The king rose. "Who is that young man?" he asked.

"It is Young John from the town," the people told him.

"Very well. Young John," said the king, as John and Atalanta stood before him, exhausted and jubilant from their efforts. "You have not won the race, but you have come closer to winning than any man here. And so I give you the prize that was promised—the right to marry my daughter."

Young John smiled at Atalanta, and she smiled back. "Thank you, sir," said John to the king, "but I could not possibly marry your daughter unless she wished to marry me. I have run this race for the chance to talk with Atalanta, and, if she is willing, I am ready to claim my prize."

Atalanta laughed with pleasure. "And I," she said to John, "could not possibly marry before I have seen the world. But I would like nothing better than to spend the afternoon with you."

Then the two of them sat and talked on the grassy field, as the crowds went away. They ate bread and cheese and purple plums. Atalanta told John about her telescopes and her pigeons, and John told Atalanta about his globes and his studies of geography. At the end of the day, they were friends.

On the next day, John sailed off to discover new lands. And Atalanta set off to visit the great cities.

By this time, each of them has had wonderful adventures, and seen marvelous sights. Perhaps some day they will be married, and perhaps they will not. In any case, they are friends. And it is certain that they are both living happily ever after.

The Sun and the Moon

by Elaine Laron
drawing by Lisa Antupit, age 14

The Sun is filled with shining light
It blazes far and wide
The Moon reflects the sunlight back
But has no light inside.

I think I'd rather be the Sun
That shines so bold and bright
Than be the Moon, that only glows
With someone else's light.

Afterword

I've often thought there ought to be a manual to hand to little kids, telling them what kind of planet they're on, why they don't fall off it, how much time they've probably got here, how to avoid poison ivy, and so on. I tried to write one once. It was called *Welcome to Earth.* But I got stuck on explaining why we don't fall off the planet. Gravity is just a word. It doesn't explain anything. If I could get past gravity, I'd tell them how we reproduce, how long we've been here, apparently, and a little bit about evolution. And one thing I would really like to tell them about is cultural relativity. I didn't learn until I was in college about all the other cultures, and I should have learned that in the first grade. A first grader should understand that his or her culture isn't a rational invention; that there are thousands of other cultures and they all work pretty well; that all cultures function on faith rather than truth; that there are lots of alternatives to our own society. Cultural relativity is defensible and attractive. It's also a source of hope. It means we don't have to continue this way if we don't like it.

—*Kurt Vonnegut, Jr.*

Authors and Composers

JUDY BLUME ("The Pain and The Great One"). Ms. Blume began writing for children in 1967. Her books include *Are You There God, It's Me, Margaret; Then Again, Maybe I Won't; It's Not the End of the World; Tales of a Fourth Grade Nothing* and *Otherwise Known as Sheila the Great.*

LUCILLE CLIFTON ("Three Wishes"). A poet and children's writer, Ms. Clifton is the author of *Good Times*—a collection of poems—and the children's books *The Boy Who Didn't Believe in Spring, Some of the Days of Everett Anderson, The Black BC's* and *Everett Anderson's Christmas Coming.*

HERB GARDNER ("How I Crossed the Street for the First Time All By Myself"). Mr. Gardner began his career as a cartoonist and creator of the "Nebbishes." He wrote the play and screenplay "A Thousand Clowns," the screenplay "Who Is Harry Kellerman and Why Is He Saying Those Terrible Things About Me" and the play and screenplay "The Goodbye People." He also wrote the novel *A Piece of the Action* and several short stories.

DAN GREENBURG ("Don't Dress Your Cat in an Apron" and "My Dog Is a Plumber"). Mr. Greenburg's best-known books are *How To Be a Jewish Mother* and *Scoring: A Sexual Memoir,* but he also wrote a children's book called *Jumbo the Boy and Arnold the Elephant.*

CAROL HALL ("Parents Are People," "It's All Right To Cry" and "Glad To Have a Friend Like You"). Ms. Hall's songs have been sung by Barbra Streisand, Neil Diamond, Shirley Bassey, Miriam Makeba and Mabel Mercer. In addition, she has recorded two albums of her own material.

SHELDON HARNICK ("Housework" and lyric for "William's Doll"). Mr. Harnick has written the lyrics for many Broadway and off-Broadway revues and musicals, among them "Fiddler on the Roof," "Fiorello," "The Apple Tree" and "The Rothschilds." He also wrote the lyrics for the theme song of the film "Heartbreak Kid."

BRUCE HART (lyrics for "Free To Be . . . You and Me" and "Sisters and Brothers"). Mr. Hart won an Emmy Award as one of the original writers for educational TV's "Sesame Street" series. He was also the lyricist for its title song. He contributed two films to "The Psychology Today Film Series." With Stephen Lawrence, he co-produced the musical portions of the record "Free To Be . . . You and Me." And he wrote the lyric for the theme from the film "Bang the Drum Slowly."

JOYCE (GLASSMAN) JOHNSON ("The Old Woman Who Lived in a Shoe"). Ms. Johnson's first novel, *Come and Join the Dance,* was published in 1962. She is a Senior Editor at the McGraw-Hill Book Company.

ELAINE LARON ("What Are Little Boys Made Of?", "No One Else" and "The Sun and the Moon"). As Writer and Head Lyricist for educational TV's series "The Electric Company," Ms. Laron wrote the lyrics for more than thirty of its songs. She has also written and produced several anti-war records, including "Hell, No, I Ain't Gonna Go!"

STEPHEN LAWRENCE (music for "Free To Be . . . You and Me," "When We Grow Up" and "Sisters and Brothers"). Mr. Lawrence's songs have been recorded by Petula Clark, Cass Elliot, Helen Reddy, Diana Ross, The New Seekers and others. His original film scores include "Jennifer On My Mind," "Hurry Up or I'll Be Thirty" and "Bang the Drum Slowly." With Bruce Hart, he co-produced the musical portions of the record "Free To Be . . . You and Me." He arranged the music for this book.

BETTY MILES ("Atalanta"). Ms. Miles has written many children's books, including *A House for Everyone* and *Just Think.* She teaches children's literature at Bank Street College of Education.

SHELLEY MILLER ("When We Grow Up"). An English major who turned to singing and song-writing, Ms. Miller has been working with Stephen Lawrence for several years. She plans to write more album material and musicals.

CARL REINER (co-author "Boy Meets Girl"). Mr. Reiner has gained fame as an actor, writer, director, producer and recording star. He won two Emmy Awards for his work on the Sid Caesar shows and six as producer and writer of the Dick Van Dyke series. His writings include the novel *Enter Laughing* and the films "The Thrill of It All" and "The Art of Love."

PHIL RESSNER ("Dudley Pippin and the Principal"). In addition to his book of *Dudley Pippin* stories, from which the selection in this book is adapted, Mr. Ressner wrote the children's books *August Explains, Jerome, At Night* and *The Park in the City.* He is working on a sequel to *Dudley Pippin.*

MARY RODGERS (music for "William's Doll" and adaptation of "Ladies First"). A composer and writer, Ms. Rodgers composed the score for the Broadway musical "Once Upon a

Mattress." She and her mother, Dorothy Rodgers, co-authored the book *A Word to the Wives* and co-author a monthly column in *McCall's* Magazine. Her children's books include *The Rotten Book* and *Freaky Friday.*

ANNE ROIPHE ("The Field"). Author of *Digging Out, Up the Sandbox* and *Long Division,* Ms. Roiphe is also a journalist and contributor to *The New York Times.*

SHEL SILVERSTEIN ("Helping" and "Ladies First"). Mr. Silverstein is an artist, cartoonist, writer, jazz singer and composer. His books for children include *The Giving Tree; Lafcadio, the Lion Who Shot Back* and *A Giraffe and a Half.* Among his most popular songs are "Sylvia's Mother," "A Boy Named Sue" and "Freakin' at the Freaker's Ball."

LINDA SITEA ("Zachary's Divorce"). An artist and writer, Ms. Sitea studied in California and New York. "Zachary's Divorce" is her first published story.

PETER STONE (co-author "Boy Meets Girl"). Mr. Stone won the Tony Award and New York Drama Critics Award for "1776," an Academy Award for "Father Goose," an Emmy Award for "The Defenders" and the Mystery Writers of America Award for "Charade."

JUDITH VIORST ("The Southpaw"). Ms. Viorst has published six children's books and three books of poetry, including *It's Hard To Be Hip Over Thirty and Other Tragedies of Married Life.* She writes a monthly column for *Redbook* magazine.

CHARLOTTE ZOLOTOW (The book *William's Doll,* from which the selection in this book is adapted). Ms. Zolotow is the author of more than fifty children's books, among them *The Quarreling Book, The Hating Book* and *The Three Funny Friends.*

Illustrators

BARBARA BASCOVE: "The Field," "Atalanta," "Three Wishes," "Zachary's Divorce"

GUY BILLOUT: "When We Grow Up," "The Pain and The Great One," "Sisters and Brothers"

DONNA BROWN: "Free To Be . . . You and Me," "Ladies First," "The Old Woman Who Lived in a Shoe," "How I Crossed the Street"

DAVID CHALK: "Glad To Have a Friend Like You"

JOHN PAUL ENDRESS: "Boy Meets Girl," "William's Doll," "It's All Right to Cry"

ARNOLD LOBEL: "Dudley Pippin and the Principal"

DOUG TAYLOR: "Don't Dress Your Cat in an Apron," "Housework," "My Dog Is a Plumber"